Titan Code

Dawn
of
Genesis

By Rey Clark

ISBN-13: 978-1796751802

Contents

1

Tessa's heart felt as though it was beating against her rib cage screaming for air. She expected for her chest to burst open at a moment's notice. She was trying her best to control her breathing, but the polluted air restricted the quality of what she took into her lungs. A scarf tightly around her nose and mouth filtered out some of the toxins but wasn't the perfect method of prevention or protection. Her feet hammered on the ally pavement. Her shoe soles were worn offering little cushion, but nothing was new anymore.

She had to make due with the limited resources available. She chugged forward in pursuit of two wanted thieves determined to catch them and see justice fulfilled. They had a significant head start, but Tessa had her customized tech to help her bridge that gap quickly and efficiently.

Tessa leaped atop an abandoned car and slid across the hood. Her feet slammed to the ground on the other side, and without hesitation, her sprint continued. "Activate Scout," she commanded aloud. A small drone detached from the outside of her backpack and hovered above her matching her pace. "Scout, find my thieves and select an optimal route." The drone flew out ahead of her, and she pressed a button on the outside of her goggles. She could hear the faint sound of buzzing as the tech came online but it took only a split second for the goggles to load and sync with Scout.

Tessa continued to the run down the alley dodging refuse and obstacles in her way. Ahead the alleyway was blocked with a massive pile of rubble from a nearby brick wall which had collapsed. The goggles measured her speed and velocity to determine a point of trajectory that would launch her over the debris with the least amount of exerted effort. Tessa needed to conserve her energy to keep her stamina in the sweltering arid heat. The goggles highlighted the precise spot on the still standing wall of the building adjacent and outlined the desired path. Tessa planted

2

her foot directly in the digitally marked spot and pushed off in the direction indicated by the goggles. She soared over the rubble and landed perfectly on the other side continuing her pursuit.

Scout began to upload a customized digital map in the corner of her goggle's display and indicated the location of the thieves with two red dots also running through the alleyways. Then the tech outlined the ideal path to catch the thieves with a dotted blue line. The most effective route was over the tops of the buildings, but she had no time to stop running and climb. "Scout, I need target coordinates for a skyhook." Tessa continued on the best footpath until the drone could solve her problem and find a quick, efficient way to the top of the buildings.

The drone compiled data and indicated two points of contact within her path up ahead. One was a tall building with a water tower on top to her left, and the other was a lower building top with a radio tower to the right of the alley. Tessa pulled an odd gun-like object out of a holster on her left thigh and pressed the power button. "Scout, send data to the skyhook." As she turned the corner and the water tower came into view on her left, she aimed the skyhook in the general direction and pulled the trigger. From the wide barrel, a metal dart with a trailing rope hurtled from the gun. The metal dart on the end split off, one headed for the water tower and the other for the radio tower atop the building across the alleyway but the rope in the center stayed connected to both with a metal eye around the master zip line she just created. With the two darts securely anchored on opposite sides of the alleyway, Tessa pulled the trigger again, and the rope connecting her to the middle of the zip line began to retract and pull her up into the air.

It was a speedy ascent, and Tessa was launched from the cool shade of the alley and into the blazing sun up over the building tops. She could feel the heat hit her like a wave of energy as she crested the rooftops. Her goggles immediately recognized the intense sunlight and shaded her eyes from the blinding light. The water tower was positioned higher than the radio tower so once Tessa reached the highest point and contacted with the zip line, she pulled the trigger again and began to slide down the path toward the radio tower building top. The wind blew past her as she descended and it cooled her off a bit. She was still blazing hot from her run, and her heart was still racing, but the brief pause gave her a quick moment to rest and regain her breath.

Just as she thought she was in the clear, Tessa felt the line shutter and began to feel slack in the line. She looked over her shoulder to see the deteriorating water tower start to topple. In a small fit of panic, Tessa pulled her legs up toward her chest hoping she could clear the side of the building before the tower fell. Once over the solid ground of the rooftop, she pulled the trigger again and the skyhook detached from the zip line, and Tessa's feet fell to the ground with a thud. She rolled forward over her right shoulder and returned to her feet. Without skipping a beat, her running resumed. The brief rest as she soared through the sky was over. She could hear the falling water tower behind her crashing over the side of the building, and its contents were spilling into the alleyway. She had dodged a bullet on that one.

Tessa continued to move in the direction of her targets still sprinting through the alleys on the virtual map transmitted to her goggles. Now that she was on the rooftops she no longer had to run around the buildings. She could run across the tops of them in a more direct route. She should easily be able to make up the distance between herself and the thieves. Tessa leaped from building top to building top and tiptoed across narrow ledges. Her long braided ponytail beat against her back and shoulders, and she ran and jumped along the rooftops. She tried not think too hard about the distance to the ground. There was no time to second guess. She relied on her scout drone to tell her if there was a gap beyond her leaping capacity.

Tessa was closing in fast, and Scout had already identified an exit strategy to return to the ground. When she reached that point, she jumped down over the building edge and planted her feet on a rusted iron escape ladder landing. Tessa paused for a brief moment waiting to see if the structure would hold or whether it would crumble away. She peered over the edge to see the two thieves running below the ladder. They had

6

heard the clanging noise of her landing and peered up at her with a surprised look on their faces. Tessa straddled the fire escape ladder and sprung the latch. The ladder slid down toward the ground. She hung on as the bottom of the ladder as it slammed to the ground, and she slid the rest of the way down with her arms and legs positioned on the outside of the ladder. She was now right on their tail, and she would overtake them soon.

The two thieves were only slightly smaller than her, and they were both younger boys. She had figured as much. The scavengers in this area often used children to do most of their dirty work. They counted on people being less inclined to shoot kids, but that didn't always pan out. This world was a kill or be killed world and people would not hesitate to take out a kid if they felt compelled to do so and mainly if it was a threat to their survival. Tessa just wanted what they had taken, and that was all, she only used force when necessary to ensure her self-preservation.

The two boys thought they were clever by scaling a ten-foot chain link gate and dropping to the

7

other side. One of them continued to run, but the other stopped to look back at Tessa approaching the fence. She saw a smirk on his face as he thought the gate would slow her or even stop her. He was naïve in his assumption. Tessa scaled the gate effortlessly and using her upper body strength pushed herself up and over the top. She fell to the ally floor bending her knees as she hit the ground to cushion her fall. The boy now had a surprised and worried look on his face. His moment of hesitation to celebrate was his downfall. Tessa was now in striking distance, and the boy knew he wouldn't be able to run from her now.

So he stood to fight, pulling a knife and waiting for her to attack. She had no desire to fight if she didn't have to, "Give back what you stole from me and I'll let you walk away."

He didn't seem interested in taking her up on the deal, so Tessa figured the only option was to take back what was rightfully hers by force. She moved in and circled him looking for that opening to strike. Tessa lunged in a couple of times to shake him and create her moment, and when the window presented itself, she acted fast. With a right-hand jab, she socked him in the jaw, and he stumbled back, but Tessa continued to move forward. This time she grabbed his knife hand and squeezed applying just enough pressure in the right pressure point to make him drop his weapon. This fight was unfair. Most of these vagabond children did not receive the same combat training as she had and that was why they preferred to run rather than fight.

The scavenger kids ran coordinated strikes on the farmers' markets sending in multiple kids at the same time. At the same moment, the kids would grab anything and everything they could get their hands on and bolt. The object of the game wasn't to pull in a big load but more a game of probability. If they're split up in different directions, they would be harder to chase. The hope was that at least some of them would get away with the stolen goods. The unlucky ones faced uncertain fates. Some are captured and beaten. Others end up on the wrong side of a gun barrel.

Tessa thought she had the runt squashed, but she underestimated the urchins. She should have known better. They played dirty and always had a trick

9

up their sleeves. She felt the strong thud of something hard on the back of her head, and she went down. The second thief had attacked her from behind. She figured he was long gone, but she was wrong had returned for his buddy. He wasted no time in pursuing his friend's attacker and started kicking her in the face and stomach as hard as he could manage. Tessa focused through the dizziness from the blow to the head and grabbed one of his legs yanking it out from underneath him. The first boy tried to wiggle toward his dropped knife, and as he reached it, Tessa scrambled to disarm him again. The boy jumped on top of her and slammed her back to the ground. He tried to use his body weight to press the blade toward Tessa's throat, but she held his forearm at bay. She used her legs to push him up and over her head slamming him to the ground and twisting the knife from his hand yet again.

She sprung up from the ground just before the second one scrambled to attack again. By now Tessa was thoroughly pissed off, and she wasn't playing games with these two. She was out for blood. As one ran toward her, Tessa met him halfway with a fury of blows from fists and feet alike, and she landed one punch hard enough to knock him out cold. She could hear the other one coming up behind her, but she wasn't falling for that one again.

He skidded to a stop trying to reverse direction as she drew her Beretta and he was now face to face with a barrel of the gun. Tessa planted her foot deep into the center of his chest which forced him to the ground landing on his backside. Tessa towered over the boy the Beretta aimed fiercely at his forehead, "My stuff, now. I won't ask a second time."

He pulled the pack from his back and slide it toward her and Tessa collect it, slinging it over her back but never once did she take her eyes off of him. Tessa learned long ago to trust no one. Turn your back on no one; unless you wanted to end up dead. Tessa backed away slowly checking briefly over her shoulder to make sure his friend remained unconscious. He also had a pack, and she intended on collecting it as well.

After she collected all of her stolen items, she addressed her captive "You're lucky I caught you. Some of the people in this town wouldn't think twice about shooting to kill."

He was still shaky, "You're not going to kill me?

"There aren't many of us who survive out here anyway. I don't intend to contribute to the problem, but you need to find another way to live." Off in the distance, she heard gunshots, "Or else you might end up like your friends." Tessa figured some of his cohorts found themselves on the wrong end of a gun held by someone who didn't think the same as Tessa. Kill or be killed.

"What am I supposed to do? My parent don't have an assigned position with H.I.V.E; they're radicals. They say H.I.V.E is evil."

"I don't believe in all the H.I.V.E does, but it has to be better than the way you're living. Sure there are rules in the H.I.V.E, but there's protection as well. It's a tradeoff. You can't steal from people and expect that it won't catch up to you in the end. Because it will. Sign on with H.I.V.E, come to school and test into a job. Sooner rather than later, before you end up dead."

"My parents would kill me."

"Or society kills you; you choose by what hand you want to die. Make a choice and take care of yourself. No one else is going to do it for you. Not even your parents. They're not looking out for your best interests now by sending you out to die. They're going to get you killed. For what? For a belief that someone other and H.I.V.E is going to step out of thin air and save the world. We're all on our own here."

"Where should I go?"

"Honestly move on to the next town and pledge to the H.I.V.E. You've burned your bridges here. I doubt it would be safe at this point."

She pulled a few ears of corn from one of the backpacks and tossed them on the ground next to him, "What's this for?"

"Consider it my gift to you. Take it and go make yourself a better life."

2

That unrelenting flaming ball of fire in the sky scorched down on the dusty plains. Tessa could feel the sweat beading on her forehead and the back of her neck. She wasn't moving much at all after her strenuous pursuit of the thieves, but it didn't matter. The air was stifling, and thick humidity hung heavy in the summer air. The harsh heat was terrible and oppressive, but over the years people had adapted to it and managed to survive. There were only two choices; adapt or die. It was a rough life, and many had perished here unless they possess the ingenuity to adjust and maintain life.

Tessa had returned the stolen corn to their stand, and her brother noticed she was a touch short. He nodded his shaggy brown head in acceptance. A few ears of corn wasn't going to break them. It was a duty to humanity and charity was something this place could use more of. It was part of being a decent person. Had the boys stolen from anyone else out here, the outcome could have been entirely different. Tessa and her brother Andy were lucky enough to have a successful family farm. Farming in this harsh environment was a challenge, and it took hard work, determination, and smarts to run a stable agricultural operation.

Tessa sat on the tailgate of the families rusty red pickup while her brother managed their produce booth. She swung her feet listening to her tunes with her earbuds. Tessa took a few moments to relax after her romp through the wreckage of Stillwater. She deserved a few moments to herself.

Andy was her older brother by about five years and after he finished his education years ago and he tested into the agricultural sector to continue the family business. Tessa and Andy made a good team, and she wanted to follow in her brother's footsteps remaining here with her family. It wouldn't be long before Andy would find a wife and start his own family. He would then inherit the farm once their father was no longer capable of the task.

Tessa's job at the market was to trade their family goods for other goods or services. She had fresh corn to barter for whatever she might find at the market. She could swap on anything from clothes and shoes to guns and ammo. It just depended on what the scavengers had managed to uncover in the rubble of once great cities, and what the family needed.

Tessa strolled down the ally of the farmers market, a ragtag string of roadside stands with crude covers to shelter the owners from the suns harsh rays. There was little wind, so even under the canopies, the relief from the humidity was non-existent. It was just hot everywhere with no hope of escaping.

Nothing was new anymore, and so the clothing choices were always worn and dingy from being buried underneath the skeletal remains of what was once Oklahoma City, which was now a pile of junk fading to dust under the crushing weight of the elements. Mother Earth was reclaiming the big cities.

Tessa managed to find a few good parts digging deep into a scavenger's bin. They all knew her to be a competent mechanic, and for that reason, her family produced good crop yields year after year. She was imaginatively intuitive and adaptable, and she was able to repurpose machines to suit farming needs.

One of the scavengers tried to wave her over and sell her a new assault rifle, but she was partial to the one she currently owned slung over her back on a strap. She did trade for some ammo but wasn't interested in much else the vendor had to offer. She had all the weapons she needed, besides they never wanted corn as payment. They always wanted her goggles or scout drone. She had custom engineered her eyewear to be useful for a wide array of tactical purposes. She never let anyone know what they were capable of; it was a secret she would take to her grave. That didn't stop people from noticing that when she was wearing the goggles, she never missed a shot, and she could gauge targets from far off distances with ease. The specs weren't up for trade, but that didn't mean she wasn't solicited week after week about them. In fact, they were her most cherished possession, second to her assault rifle. She had built tiny earbuds into the goggles so that she could listen to her favorite tunes from a scavenged electronic sound box. Music gave her peace in a world surrounded by turmoil.

Tessa was almost always unsentimental to most material objects. In this world, it was best not to become too attached to anything or anyone for that matter. But the site of her favorite vendor Minnie quickly brought a smile to her face. Minnie was an older middle-aged widower. Tessa was surprised by her longevity in this environment, although the wear and tear on her body was visually apparent. She was older than most that survived in this wilderness. The sun and wind had ravaged her skin and taken a toll on her body. Her hair was white with her showing age, and she had trouble moving around. But somehow she managed to survive on her own and kept an overwhelmingly positive attitude despite the miserable life she had lived. Her husband and sons had passed years ago but some way she managed to endure. Tessa figured it was pure stubbornness that she refused to let go. She had the willpower of a titan and for that Tessa admired her. Tessa had volunteered her time in the past to rig up some home protections for Minnie in hopes to keep her safe. She was a wise treasure that Tessa wasn't ready to lose to this awful hell hole.

Minnie dressed in her typical patch worked tattered overalls, attending her market booth. She had her precious Peck sitting on her right shoulder as she worked. Peck was a rooster who perched on her shoulder wearing a pair of makeshift pants to prevent droppings from soiling Minnie's shoulder. Wherever Minnie was Peck wasn't far behind, and for a simple-minded rooster, he had a personality larger than life. He thought he was a person and better than most. A rooster with a chip on his shoulder, if that makes any sense. Logically, Minnie traded eggs at her booth.

Tessa couldn't help but stop by Minnie's booth, "Good afternoon Minnie."

She smiled in response, "Tessa dear, how are you today?"

"Hot." She fanned herself with a hand.

"Amen child. It's a real scorcher today." Peck squawked at her and Minnie hushed him.

"Can I trade for a few eggs?"

"Sure can. How many would you like?"

"A dozen." Tessa laid out a bundle of corn on the table in exchange.

"Tessa that's too much." She tried to push some back to her. She didn't want Tessa to overpay.

"I don't mind Minnie. We love your eggs." Tessa pulled a few kernels of corn off of an ear and fed them to Peck, and he quickly stopped squawking to feed his face.

"I couldn't accept dear. If you want to help out, you could look at the old truck. It's not running right, and you're the best mechanic 'round these parts."

Tessa pressed a finger to her lips, "Shh don't tell anyone. Let's keep that our little secret." Tessa winked, and Minnie smiled. Minnie knew that Tessa liked to keep her talents hidden.

Tessa walked around behind Minnie's booth to the rusty old pickup truck. She opened the driver's door and popped the hood. Minnie tossed her the key, and Tessa cranked the engine. She could hear it whine as the engine struggled to turn over. It was a simple fix. Minnie gave her a few eggs to barter for parts, and Tessa added some corn to sweeten the deal. She wanted to make sure she got a good quality alternator that was going to last. It didn't take long, and Tessa had the vehicle starting with ease. She took a few moments to tune up the engine, and before long she had it humming as well as was possible for such an old hunk of junk.

As she was finishing up, she shuddered at a loud and familiar sound. The sirens in Stillwater sang the tune of warning and the commerce of the market halted immediately. Minnie looked at Tessa, "What is it?"

Tessa climbed up into the truck bed and onto the top of the cab to see into the distance beyond the main street of town. She pulled on her goggles and focused them on the horizon. "Dust storm…" She focused again on some figures out in front of the storm. There were several utility vehicles and motorcycles, and they didn't have the look of friendlies. "Looks like a gang is riding into town ahead of the storm."

As if on cue, one of the town scouts rode into the market on a motorcycle. He told the attendants that the Dust Devil Gang was riding in front of the storm. They were a notorious gang in these parts. Although they had not been to Stillwater, their reputation preceded them. They were best known for using dust storms for cover. As people were hunkered down for shelter from the wind, they pillaged what they could unimpeded by local citizens.

Tessa jumped down from the truck and helped Minnie load up as fast as she could, "You get home and lock yourself in that panic room. Don't open that door for anyone or anything."

She hugged Tessa, "Be safe."

Tessa answered smugly, "Come on Minnie. You know what happens when people pick a fight with me."

Tessa returned to her family's booth to find her brother had most of the merchandise already loaded in their truck, "Sorry, I was helping Minnie."

"I figured. We better head out. You wanna work ahead and put the farm on lockdown."

"I'm on it." Tessa kick-started the engine of her rugged dirt bike, pulled her goggles down, affixed a handkerchief over her nose and mouth and selected a tune for the ride, *Back in the Saddle Again* by a group named Aerosmith. She rode out ahead to warn the family and secure the farm. Lucky for them the farm was on the opposite side of town, so they had a little more time to prepare than some others.

3

It was a quick ride to the farmhouse, where Tessa warned her mother and sister Evie to secure the house and seek the fortified shelter in the basement. She rode the dirt bike out to the cornfield in search of her father. She weaved in and out of cornrows and access roads until she reached him to deliver the warning. He needed to bring the equipment in and help protect the farm. His instructions to her were to protect the crops and man the lookout nest. It was her usual position when the farm went on lockdown.

Tessa had engineered some custom security features in addition to added protections for the family and crops. The plants were the most precious commodity they had on the farm second only to the family. They had some livestock which her brother would secure in the barn, but she had other unique contraptions to protect the fields from the elements including dust storms. Their livelihood depended on successful crop yield.

The most intense dust storms came from the southwest, so Tessa had rigged precautions to protect the crops from ravaging wind and abrasive dust coming from that direction. She rode her dirt bike up along the far west edge of the field and picked up a tire iron she had strategically placed on the southern-most fence post. As she rode back toward the farmhouse along the side of the cropland, she struck some intermittent metal pylons fixated in the ground. As these targets were triggered, large metal plates sprung up from the ground to sit perpendicular to the ground and flush with the fence serving as a solid blockade. The metal plates were roughly the height of the corn stocks and would shield some of the crops from being torn from the soil in the high wind gusts. It wouldn't save them all, but it would save enough.

At the end of the field and adjacent to the barn, Tessa stopped the bike at the foot of a tall metal scaffolding tower. At one time these towers were used to send signals to electrical devices around the world.

Now they were just broken monuments; forgotten to the ravages of time. She opened a metal box at the base of the tower which housed a motor she had repurposed to her needs. Tessa primed the engine and pulled the recoil starter rope to awaken the motor. Once it was purring, she pulled a lever, and a chain of events moved from the motor housing out along the ground just under the metal plates protecting the field and stretching for miles along the field line. The motor was the catalyst for pneumatic valves Tessa had positioned along the length of the field and strung together as a chained reaction. The pneumatic valves launched a pressurized projectile into the air angled over the acreage. Behind the weighed missiles a thin muslin cloth rippled through the air.

Tessa designed the entire apparatus in two parts. The metal sheeting was to slow the force of the wind and redirect it upward thus sparing the crops from being torn to shreds. The launched muslin covered the majority of the field and protected the plants from the falling dust. As the wind hit the metal and shot upward, it carried substantial amounts of debris, and as dirt settled on the leaves, it prevented the ability for sunlight to reach the plant. Many crops withered and died because of this phenomenon. Later the family could remove the muslin cloth along with the thick layer of dust after the storm, and the plants escape the grim fate, and her family had food to eat and to sell. The whole system was cumbersome, but it worked. She hated to deploy because that meant she would have to reload it later.

The storm currently on its way was immense, and there was no other option but to use her contraption. With the Dust Devil Gang out in front of the wind and using the dust for cover as they vandalized locals, she would get the chance to use some of her other inventions as well. She had rigged the entire farm with all manner of security devices. The locals had heard rumor of their farm's security, but they did an excellent job of keeping the details hidden and secret. It was just best to have some cards up your sleeve in case a plan goes sideways. Tessa also didn't want people to know the extent of her mechanical and technical knowledge.

Next stop was a visit to the crow's nest to watch the storm roll into town along with its companions. Tessa threaded her left wrist into a roped loop attached to a cable wire running from the bottom of the tower to the top platform. She wrapped her hand around the cable for an extra tight hold and kicked a nearby lever which activated a pulley system sending her hurtling upward to the top of the tower at maximum velocity. Tessa cleared about halfway, and her abruptly ascent halted. She squinted to see what the problem was at the top of the tower. It seemed that the pulley was stuck. Equipment often malfunctioned as a result of the harsh environment. The dirt and grim got into everything and caused all kinds of problems. She bounced a couple of times dangling precariously above the ground. After a couple of jerks, she got the system moving again and arrived at the top of the tower.

Tessa nestled down and rearranged her belongings, pulling her assault rifle around front. She pulled the gun up and pointed toward the approaching storm. The scope pressed against her right eye and she closed the left focusing into the distance. The wind was raging forward and on its way toward Stillwater. She could barely make out the figures of the Dust Devil Gang out in front. She switched to her goggles and magnified the image until she could make out more details. She wanted to assess what they might be up against if it came to a fight. She counted two off-road Jeeps, one van, and about five motorcycles. It was hard to say precisely how many gang members there were but by her approximation, there was around a dozen. That was enough to cause a heap of problems for the people of Stillwater. They could target family farms along their path, which made Tessa's home a potential target.

She pulled a walkie out of the steel box she affixed to the top of the tower for supplies. "I'm betting there's about a dozen of them give or take."

Her father answered, "How far?"

She selected a different function on her goggles to judge distance, "About a mile out from town."

"We're all prepped down here. You ready?"

"I'm ready."

29

The sky turned darker as the storm moved across the horizon obscuring the sun and Tessa could see the bandits arrive in town just before the storm. They broke into what houses and shops were occupied, looting and murdering as they went along. There wasn't much Tessa could do for those who didn't have the means to protect themselves and their belongings. Some people were better prepared for the worse case scenario than others. Tessa had made several efforts to protect their assets, and she had a feeling her systems could be put to the test in the next few minutes.

It took only moments for the storm to overtake the gang and they now worked under cover of the dust storm. Although it was hard to see, Tessa had tools at her disposal. Her goggles equipped with an infrared function could peer through the clouds of swirling dust and show the outlines of heat signatures. She had positioned sensors throughout the farm so she would know where people were and in what direction they moved. She pulled out the control panel pad so she could monitor those sensors. Pulling her scarf up to cover her mouth she waited, anticipating the gang to leave town and strike some homesteads along their exit path.

Tessa watched as they moved out of town in the same direction as the storm. Unfortunately, that put their farm directly in the path. She watched from infrared as the gang traveled down the dirt road. Their caravan slowed to a crawl on the dirt road as they canvased the farm. From the look of the crops and house, they targeted the farm with raiding potential and turned down the farm driveway.

Tessa readied her EMP burst on the control panel. She had to time it just right to hit the van. She figured the van housed all their comm links and other electronics. At least that would be where she would put all the communication equipment if she ran the gang. They were in the middle of a dust storm, and that would be the vehicle which offered the most protection for sensitive electronic equipment. Tactically, she needed to cut them off so they would be flying blind in the dust storm, giving her home field advantage.

Midway down the road, she blew the roadside EMP, and the van slowed to a crawl and eventually halted. Now the bandits knew someone was watching and had the means to derail their operation. They would be less than pleased she decommissioned their equipment and stopped their caravan.

A few gang members remained behind to service the van, but the remaining bandits moved toward the farm. They now had a score to settle. Tessa initiated another protocol. With the press of a button, road spikes emerged from the dirt driveway puncturing the tires of one of the Jeeps and two of the motorcycles. The impact sent the two motorcyclists over the handlebars as they lost control on the loose gravel. Four more bandits down. She still had about five more headed in the direction of the house.

Tessa stood against the raging storm winds and gripped a zip-line wire tethered to the barn behind the farmhouse. She put her equipment back in the steel container and slung her rifle over her back. There was no more she could accomplish from this vantage point. "We're down to five on the move...flying the roost."

"Copy." Her father's voice confirmed, "We are ready for contact."

"Hold the door."

"Be safe."

Tessa zipped out of the tower and down to the barn loft. She approached her barn command control equipment and turned a few knobs prepping to send signals to some charges set around the house. She picked up a remote, detonator and blasting cap just in case things went south and shoved it in her pocket along with some extra magazines for her rifle and sidearm. Goggles on, she peaked out the barn loft down to the yard behind the house. She could see a figure on infrared sneaking along the back side of the house. She aimed the rifle, and when she had him square in her sights, she gently squeezed the trigger. The bullet found its mark and the body fell lifeless to the ground. It wasn't her first kill. Tessa had taken life before, and it wouldn't be her last. She would never be comfortable with ending a life, but in this world, there often wasn't much choice. There was little room for hesitation or contemplation, and there was undoubtedly little compassion.

Her shot rang out and alerted the rest of the Dust Devil Gang that there were people here that were going to put up a fight. She could see them on the infrared scramble to action. They took cover behind trees, the woodpile and the farm truck. She could hear them yelling but couldn't make out what they were saying. The whipping winds from the dust storm made it impossible for her to listen, but it also made it impossible for them to hear each other. Without comms, they were cut off from the groups that were left behind to tend to downed equipment. Confusion was just what Tessa was hoping to cause. I gave her the window she needed.

"Backdoor is clear. They're all out front. One behind the truck, two behind the big oaks and one behind the woodpile."

"I don't want to shoot up my truck." Her brother's concern over old red was admissible in their situation, but if she could salvage the truck, she would try.

"I can get to the truck if you guys can cover."

Tessa moved from the loft to the barn door and slipped outside, no longer protected from the storm winds. She struggled to maneuver in the winds but remained focused on traversing around behind the tree line and to where the enemy crouched behind the truck. He was shouting orders to the others in between suppressive fire from Tessa's father and brother. She slung her rifle over her back drawing her expandable batons. They wanted to spare the truck from bullet holes, so this was her only option. She moved in slowly letting the goggles lead the way. Visibility was low, and without the goggles, she wouldn't be able to see much in front of her. Her enemy didn't have goggles like hers so he would be at a disadvantage and wouldn't know she hit him until it was too late.

She crept up behind him as he was distracted with the suppressive fire from the main farmhouse. One quick swing of her right baton to the back of his knees and he knelt down to the ground. She stepped around in front of him and with a swift backhanded left with the other baton he was knocked out cold on the ground. "Target down," she reported.

"Three more. You got em?" Her brother asked.

"Cover me."

Tessa turned on her music to focus her concentration on combat, *Enter Sandman*, Metallica. The music helped her center her mind and made her a much more efficient fighter. Her instructors hated it at first claiming it would be distracting, but it had the opposite effect on her.

Tessa moved toward her opponents ready to defend her family. Two of them from behind the trees came toward her. The third trailed behind them from the woodpile. She engaged the first two targets simultaneously. Her batons struck them hard, but they didn't back down. With a backside roundhouse kick, she hit one on the side of the head hard enough to send him to the ground. He wasn't knocked out, but he was dizzy and slow to return to his feet. She positioned herself to leverage her weigh against the other, grabbing around the neck and as she twisted around him, he flipped over her shoulder and landed hard on his back. A forceful blow to the head and he was out. The other one was up again but still wobbling. She planted her foot in his chest sending him hurling backward. The last one from the woodpile was closing in. She pulled her sidearm and with a double tap of the trigger eliminated him. She turned her handgun to the other trying to get up for the second time and pulled the trigger.

She looked around to find that the others she had decommissioned on the driveway earlier now headed toward her. Running to the aid of their comrades as they heard the gunfire erupt. Tessa disappeared in the dust storm taking cover behind one of the old oak trees. She discharged her pistol mag, reloaded and returned it to her side holster. She pulled her assault rifle from around her backside. Safety off and on the prowl; she assessed her situation.

With her head on a swivel, she moved forward sweeping her surroundings with the assault rifle at the ready. She crept from the oak tree toward the truck. The road was to the right which is where she anticipated the next attack to come from, but her brother had given her instructions not to destroy his truck with bullet holes. So she had to eliminate her targets before they could fire on her and hit the pickup so using it for a cover wasn't an option. As her marks came into view, she pulled the trigger releasing a microburst of ammo and eliminating the threat. But her forward focus had given her tunnel vision. She noticed a large body coming at her fast from her right peripheral, but it was too late for her to react.

He barreled into her full speed, and it felt like a tank hit her. He grasped the barrel of the gun and forced it toward the sky. Bullets sprayed into the air in surprise. He had managed to neutralize her weapon and backed her into the truck. He used his body weight to pin her up against the vehicle and force the assault rifle roughly into her body. He positioned the barrel across her throat and pressed down hard. She struggled to push against him, but he had mass and leverage towering over her. She wiggled and banged against the truck. She heard her brother curse over the comms, and she listened as the front door to the house swung open and slammed shut.

Andy came storming across the yard and reached into the truck bed emerging with a tire iron. He approached the man holding Tessa and swung hard busting the back of his skull open. He fell to the ground, and Tessa nodded in thanks but pulled the assault rifle back up and regained focus. Andy drew a pistol and moved in tandem with her. Two of the gang members had managed to get a couple of the decommissioned motorcycles running, and one of the jeeps wasn't far behind. They were charging Tessa and her brother traversing through the front yard. She had just about had enough of these hooligans, with a double tap her brother took out one cyclist. Tessa picked up the nearby tire iron and as the other cyclists tried to run her over she stepped to the side and nailed the rider in the chest with the tire iron sending him backward off the seat. The motorcycle fell to the ground sliding to a stop. Her brother detained the cyclist, and she picked up the bike. The jeep headed straight for her, and so she decided to play a bit of chicken. She raced toward them head on, but at the last moment, she swerved to the right. As she passed them, she tossed a cluster of explosives into the back of the jeep. Tessa fish-tailed the bike around spraying gravel from the driveway as she turned. The Jeep moved to reposition and head back toward her. She pulled the detonator from her pocket a pressed the button. A deafening boom echoed through the storm and debris sprayed in all directions, including a few mangled body parts. With a thud, a bloody arm landed on the hood of her brother's truck leaving a dent in the metal. Her brother gave her an annoyed look, and she just shrugged. It wasn't a bullet hole.

Tessa and her brother smiled at one another and then continued moving forward to the road revealing that the remaining gang members had grabbed what they could and cut loose. They cut their losses and left the farm, minus a few gang members, but they hadn't been completely wiped out, and that was a shame.

Tessa hated that these gangs roamed the countryside preying on the poor and weak. They were an unnecessary plague in addition to all of the other horrors that survivors had to face in this world. Tessa and Andy scavenged what they could from the gang attack, but he didn't have googles like hers. He could only withstand so much of the dust storm before he had to return to the house. She followed him inside to comfort her family and ride out the storm. She would have a whole lot of clean up to look forward to tomorrow morning. Hopefully, she would gain some spare parts from the mangled vehicles left behind. If she was fortunate, she might recover some new tech or at least some new electronic components to update some of her current equipment.

4

Tessa closed her eyes and let the blades of green grass tickle her toes. Her feet dangled from the wooden swing hanging from the old oak tree. She let the summer sun warm her face and the breeze blow through her long brown tresses. The sweet smells of summer filled the air with fragrant wildflowers from the rolling meadow, accompanied by the sound of water babbling in the nearby brook. She could not think of better way to spend a summer afternoon than outside in the fresh air.

She thought the day couldn't be any better and then her best friends showed up to prove that notion wrong. Arica and Sam ran through the lush fields to meet with her at the swing. Arica was a fifteen-year-old African American girl who was a genius level brainiac, and Sam was a sporty sixteen-year-old Asian American boy. These two were her closest companions, and Tessa held them both near to her heart. They had known each other since they were young and their bonds were unbreakable.

They spent the vibrant afternoon rolling in the lush green grass laughing carefree and fun. They swam in a quaint swimming hole with bright blue sparkling water and a cascading waterfall. The water was cool and inviting under the summer sun. They took turns jumping from the waterfall rocks and splashing into the refreshing water.

They were laughing and playing when they were interrupted by a faint voice, "Tessa…Tessa Jones. Could you please read the next paragraph in the textbook?"

Tessa's beautiful summer day faded away to return to the harsh reality of her school classroom. She scanned the room looking at the staring faces of her classmates. Arica mouthed the page number, and Tessa turned her text to the right page and began to read the paragraph. She had been daydreaming again which was a frequent occurrence. She could see that Mrs. Williams was annoyed by her lack of attention. There would undoubtedly be another note going home to her parents today.

Tessa couldn't help the fact that history lessons bored her. She didn't know how many more times she could stomach another reading on the Great Collapse. Since the Collapse, the education system had been forced to solicit propaganda to what few students remained. The standing reformed government, consisting of a handful of professional field leaders. They insisted that children be taught never to forget the Great Collapse and the causes that lead to the downfall of the world as it was once known. Those that remained as survivors would always remember and never repeat the mistakes of the past.

The surviving human population was currently loosely governed by a handful of professional experts in fields that serve to impact the survival of the human population. They call themselves the H.I.V.E, Human Improvement in Vitality Embassy. The leader's expert representatives in the fields of agriculture, military, medicine, engineering, and education. Together these leaders organize the remaining human population

44

through the education system. A series of tests assess both mental and physical capacity to determine what field of work children are best suited. Children are then assigned their permanent profession based on those test results. Tessa's family tested into their assigned job function in the agriculture sector, and they farmed the land formerly known as the state of Oklahoma to feed the surviving human populous.

There were many factors which lead to the Great Collapse, and lessons were designed to cover them all. The downfall began years ago when countries and their governments feared each other so much that they were willing to sacrifice everything to stay ahead of their competition. The drive for economic power led to the eventual breakdown of the Earth itself. Humans consumed all the fossil fuels and contaminated most of the drinking water. The worst was the Global Warming which was caused by pollutants destroying the protective ozone. As a result, the polar ice caps melted which in turn flooded most of the coastal areas of the world including the entire eastern seaboard of what was once the United States. Without the ozone and the ice caps, the ocean temperatures decreased, and the jet stream along with the weather patterns changed dramatically. The Earth's temperature rose to nearly unbearable levels, and those that weren't strong enough perished in the oppressive heat. Those that survived faced violent, unpredictable weather which tore apart the landscape.

If all that wasn't bad enough, while the world was crumbling, national leaders were preoccupied with their power struggles and aspirations of world domination. Governments began investing in genetic alterations in the quest to create the perfect super soldier. What they ended up with was people with genetically enhanced abilities that after time no longer wanted to be locked in a laboratory and subjected to testing. They quickly learned that their enhanced abilities made them superior to their oppressors and they rebelled against their government creators.

The governments toppled one by one by their own creations which we call "Evos," since they have evolved far beyond the typical human genome. The Evos now ruled the world on a global level, and they control vast territories. With government nearly non-existent, someone needed to pick up the pieces and lead the remains of humanity. But until that someone came along, everyone just tried their best to stay alive. So humans lived under the Evos, and as long as they don't cause any trouble then, for the most part, they leave the humans to our own business. That didn't mean that humans weren't still scared of them. Evos fought amongst each other for favored territory, and the collateral damage was often innocent humans. Evos also fought against the H.I.V.E to ensure that human domination and strength doesn't rise again to power. Everyday citizens were just helplessly stuck in between the Titans struggling for control in the crumbling world.

No longer contained, Evos mingle amongst humans and DNA can potentially mix. This problem leads to another problem. Anyone could have Evo genes and develop abilities. Children who have Evo genes, manifest abilities in adolescence. Once children in the schools reach the age of sixteen, they begin blood testing for Evo DNA genetic markers. Those that test positive are shipped away and never seen again.

Tessa preferred the imaginary world in her head, and she daydreamed as often as she could manage. She had never experienced any of the past luxuries she imagined in her daydreams. She had only read about them in the books that remain from a time long ago. The Great Collapse had happened hundreds of years ago, and all the beautiful things written in those stories had long ago become nothing but dust and memories. What remained was the shell of that world, destroyed and decaying to the sands of time. The beauty has gone from the world, and hope snuffed out. All that remained was the sheer will to survive. Hope that you might live long enough to be an adult and have a family, before being consumed by dust inhalation or an unintended victim of an Evo conflict.

Tessa finished reading her paragraph aloud to the class and then she slumped back into her chair and gazed out the window. Outside the school was a barren wasteland of dirt covered in sickly looking brown corn or soybeans plants. The sun beat down on the field with tremendous heat. The temperature made it stifling to breath when outside. The school wasn't much cooler, but at least they had a generator, and they could power some air conditioning. It was far better than the being outside.

The wind whipped across the landscape and with it dirt bombarding the window. Being outside in a wind storm was like walking through sandpaper. The high-velocity dirt was abrasive and course and required the use of face masks and goggles to prevent the dust from being inhaled or damaging the eyes. A common cause of death here was the inhalation of the dirt over an extended period that injured the lungs to the point of no repair. With all the dust and dirt flying around it was nearly impossible to keep it out of a building and that led to a buildup of grim inside every building. There was just no way to keep it out. It blew in faster than you could clean it up.

After their history lesson, they got to take a short break for lunch before combat training. Tessa preferred combat training over the mundane droning of history lessons. Since the collapse of government and the rise of Evos, there was more of a focus on self-defense. The instructors were also on the lookout for qualified candidates to assign further military training. They scouted for exceptional talent to fill their ranks of soldiers to build the slow-growing army that they could send to slaughter against Evos. Military troops could do little to defend against some of the extreme superhuman powers some of the Evos possessed. If an Evo wanted to do something, there was little to be done that could stop most of them.

Combat training was conducted both indoors and outdoors depending on the skill practiced. Tessa preferred to be indoors where the heat and dust were far less of a concern if the environment outdoors was better she might prefer the outdoor training. The indoor practice focused on tactical training and hand to hand combat. Tessa had mastered many martial arts techniques, but there were so many yet to learn. She preferred a mixed martial arts style as opposed to being restricted to one discipline. She took her favorite bits and pieces from each form and used them as she saw fit.

In addition to unarmed combat, students were also trained to fight with a variety of different melee weapons. Tessa was proficient in swords, staff, duel wielding batons, and polearms. Her favorites were the staff and the batons. She found unexpected pleasure in bludgeoning her opponents into submission. Sometimes the enjoyment concerned her, but it was just a lack of amusement that led to her satisfaction in combat training. She often wondered if there was something wrong with her mind. Perhaps her morals were warped by the hardness of her training environment. She considered the fact that she was merely desensitized to violence over the years because of everything she had witnessed in the hard reality.

Violence was a part of everyday life. Evo attacks could happen at any time and in any place. Death was something that children had to face at an early age. Young children had to consider their mortality every day. There were no safe places for anyone anymore; even children. The reality was that many people didn't live much past their forties. If they managed to survive an Evo incident, then they eventually succumbed to the many physical ailments which were becoming increasingly more common. The dusty environment caused respiratory disease, polluted water and soil led to contaminated crops that caused cancers and other illnesses. It was growing harder and harder to live in this world and living required someone to work hard to survive.

Physicians were few and far between, and medicine was a scarce resource, so there was little available to help humanity survive. People who did survive did so by their own skills and determination. It wasn't uncommon to encounter death on a daily basis. People were dying all around. Fear of death was a way of life, and many of the students at her school had already lost parents and now raised by older siblings. Society, as a result, was youthful, but illness was affecting people younger and younger. It was a vicious cycle that didn't seem like it would stop or slow any time soon.

Today Tessa's training was outdoors at the firing range where they learned to operate a variety of side arms and long arms. This tactical training was much different from hand to hand practice, and it was outside in the hot, dusty Oklahoma desert. She had to wear a face mask covering her nose and mouth to prevent the inhalation of dangerous levels of particles from the air. Her goggles protected her eyes so that she could see what she was shooting. Despite her aversion to working in the outdoor environment, she was competent in this training as well. She had to be careful not to be too proficient at military training, or she risked being shipped off to join what remained of the armed forces. Sam's older brother was shipped off to one of the infantry units, and he lasted about three months before they sent his body home to rest. Tessa had no desire to offer herself up as cannon fodder for Evos. She only wanted to be good enough to seem competent enough to protect herself and her family.

Tessa walked a fine line when it came to her strengths and weaknesses. She was good at science, and she was good at fighting, but she strategically held back just enough that she wouldn't end up in the science H.I.V.E or the armed forces. Tessa wanted to stay with her family. It was all she had ever known. Most of her family before her were farmers and Tessa had no wish for an assignment of anything or anywhere else. It scared her half to death to imagine transport to a place

53

where she knew no one. She wanted to stay where she was comfortable.

Tessa picked up her automatic rifle and loaded the weapon before entering one of the obstacle course simulations. The simulations were designed to replicate a scenario that might happen in everyday life. The objective was to work your way around the problem successfully, and that meant not getting yourself killed. The simulations weren't designed to kill anyone but in the real life situation failure to gain tactical advantage meant you ended up in a coffin. The sad reality was that even if you managed to maintain a tactical position in a fight against an Evo, you could do everything right and still end pushing up daisies. Most Evos were powerful enough to end a life with minimal effort, so the training was pretty pointless.

However, some drifters could cause problems in these parts as well, like the Dust Devils. Drifters were essentially nomads without permanent homes who roam from place to place taking whatever they want. Some drifters are kind, and people do what they can to help out, but the bad ones are armed and dangerous.

They tend to travel in groups and can quickly take over a farm if the occupants are unprepared. They kill the farmers, take what they want and move on. It happens far more often than most people like to admit. Just another reason to always watch your back. Letting your guard down for even a moment could mean a swift end, even for kids. That's why they push all the training and shove all the history lessons down their throats, but there's always that one kid who thinks that the rules don't apply and they don't last very long.

5

Once combat training was over, everyone came back inside for what the instructors termed a lunch break. Tessa liked to think of the slop as cruel and unusual punishment. They always served the blandest tasting food and nine times out of ten it was cold or soggy on top of the lack of flavor. Today wasn't any different, and Tessa tried to choke down the food for the lack of any better options. The poor choices of food was a product of their environment, and some crops had long since gone extinct. They could not grow and thrive in the current climate. H.I.V.E researchers were able to genetically engineer some crops to withstand the harsh environment, but some species became lost to time.

Tessa and her friends always sat at a table as far from the other kids as they could manage. She really couldn't stand most of the kids that attended here. It seemed like they were already being divided out into their future duties before they tested. Long ago humanity was segregated by skin color, ethnicity, or religion but all of that seemed pointless now. They had a new set of groups which hinged on individual, and collective survival and the new direction drove people to congregate in new societal groupings.

There was a table of nerdy kids who were no doubt destined to be physicians, engineers or scientists, and they looked down their noses at the rest. They saw themselves as brainiacs and future scientists, and that made them believe they were elitists. It made no sense for them to act so much better than the other kids. After all, they lived in the heart of the Ag district, and their families were farmers. Farmers were just as crucial as the scientists. Without food, scientists can't survive, regardless of how intelligent they are. Everyone needs food. Tessa couldn't stand to associate with that pretentious bunch. She wished they could see how illogical they were behaving. But why bother; they could care less.

There was a table of average kids who were probably going to continue running the family farm when it was their turn in succession. There was nothing wrong with being a farmer but it seemed like some of these kids were jealous of the others. Some of them still dreamed of being something different and living a different life. There were some of those kids that studied night and day to change their station, and some of them succeed, but the odds of breaking that mold are slim to none. The school's most considerable portion of students would most likely remain in agriculture.

The creative kids were good with their hands. There weren't very many of them, but they could be destined to be engineers or masons; building the future. At least that's what all the propaganda says, but Tessa had never seen any new buildings or inventions. She had always heard that the H.I.V.E keeps all the innovations and development for themselves and she was sure part of that was true. Logic told her that it would be silly to build new things out here where they lacked the resources to defend. That was just a beacon for some Evo to come and knock it down and she didn't desire that kind of attention around here.

Then there was the group that Tessa loved to hate, the meatheads. The group of muscle-bound morons who's collective intelligence rivaled that of a rabid dog. And that was phrasing it nicely. All this group wanted to do was to bully the rest of the kids in the school because they weren't mentally capable of contributing anything else. These were the menaces that just needed to be shipped off to slaughter. They were useful for little else.

Of course, there were those that didn't quite fit in a group. They were the fringes of society. They would either find a place or become scavengers like the young thieves in the marketplace. You either fit in, or you are forced into exile; separated from humanity.

Tessa's small group were misfits that could fit into one of the cliques but were just introverted; choosing to be separate. They wanted to avoid societies labels. They tried to keep their options open. Arica was a shy young girl with dark skin and frizzy hair. She was the smartest person Tessa knew. She excelled in math and science, and Tessa was never sure if she would make a great physician or an engineer. She could potentially be either with her range of knowledge. Sam was an Asian boy who had a gift when it came to defensive tactics. He was talented at fighting and weaponry. But Sam wasn't a meathead. He was a thinker. Sam didn't just beat someone down he studied his opponents and calculated his moves. Tessa was sure he would make an exceptional leader in the military. She only hoped the test showed his full potential and they didn't waste his skills as a meat shield on the frontlines.

The three of them got along well despite having so many differences. They could all see the big picture. All of this didn't matter. School was just a step toward something more significant, and it wasn't a step they controlled. They were pawns of a leadership that had no idea what they were doing. No one knows how to stop the Evos. And no one knows how to reverse the damage done to the earth. Everyone is equally screwed. It's a game or survival and realizing your insignificant end. Tessa admitted, it was a bleak outlook on life, but that's pretty much what everything boiled down to in the long game.

"Hey, I have a new treasure trove of parts to shuffle though tonight after school. Who's interested?"

Tessa was referring to the leftovers from Dust Devil Gang's attack on the farm.

"I have to study tonight," Arica politely decline the invite.

Sam was ready to participate, "My schedule is wide open tonight. As long as I can take a few parts for our farm equipment."

"I'm sure I have enough to share." Tessa didn't want to sort through the materials on her own if she could get people to help it would be nice.

"There's a couple parts we need. If I don't find them, will you go with me to the salvage yard?"

Tessa cringed at the idea, "I hope we find what you need at my place. I hate the salvage yard."

"Me too. That's why I want you watching my back."

The salvage yard was operated by scavengers that collected old parts and other junk from abandoned cities. They answered to Static Shock who was the resident Evo tyrant in the area. The scavengers would take whatever they could that wasn't bolted down and scrap it out. They were bull-nosed negotiators and known to be cheapskates and crooks. Not to mention that the salvage yard wasn't a secure location and open to anyone. It was hard to say who or what you might run into there. It was a dangerous place and always a last resort.

The afternoon after lunch was devoted to math and science which always made Arica happy. Tessa was proficient at both, but she made sure to hold back just enough to not be classified. She wasn't sure what job she wanted to test into, but she felt it best to keep herself in the position to swing her outcome in one direction or another. There were few choices for many of these kids, and Tessa felt empowered by having even an ounce of control over her destiny. It was probably the only time in her life she would ever be able to exert any amount of power over her life.

After school, Tessa gathered her belongings and headed outside to the pick-up area. Her older brother Andy always picked Tessa and her younger sister Evie up after he ran errands in town for the day. Sometimes he was parked there waiting for them, and other times they had to sit around and wait. It all depended on how busy his day was and what farm equipment had broken down. There weren't any more manufacturers, so whatever material already existed was what they were stuck with, and routine repair and maintenance was a way of life.

Andy often had Tessa do the machine work, and she didn't mind the challenge. He always said she was better at the repairs and sometimes she could make it work better than before. Tessa enjoyed engineering she just didn't want too many people to know. It wasn't too long ago the word got out that local handyman Tommy Blanc was an excellent mechanic and soon outsiders were bringing their equipment in for repair. It was great for business until he couldn't keep up with the demand. A desperate farmer kidnapped him and ended up killing him in the end. It was just best to keep a low profile.

Outside in the blazing heat and sandpaper wind, Tessa found Evie, and she also found Brock Turner terrorizing the other students. Brock was a meathead, and all he knew how to do was fight. Tessa couldn't wait for him to be shipped off to the infantry. She hoped that day would come sooner rather than later. He was becoming increasingly harder for the instructors to control and it was high time they pass on their problem.

On this day, he decided to pick on the wrong bookworm and Tessa wasn't in the mood to deal with any nonsense. Brock was knocking books from Arica's hands and laughing as she picked them up over and over. When she picked them up again, he smacked them back to the ground. Tessa could see Arica trying to fight back her tears and stay strong, but she was sensitive. She didn't want to show the bully weakness, but Arica was not cut out for confrontation. Lucky for her, Tessa had no problem with confronting the moron.

As she approached them, her voice boomed over the shouts of the spectators who watch idly as Brock bullied Arica, "Hey Brock. Leave her alone!"

He stopped and gave Tessa a casual glance, "Go back to the farm Jones." He shoved Arica to the ground and looked defiantly to Tessa.

She didn't expect him to obey her order; he was much too stupid for that. He was arrogant and unprepared for what she was about unleash. Tessa approached Arica and offered a hand to help her to her feet, turning her back to Brock in the process. With her back turned toward Brock, she knew what to expect. Tessa saw the movement of his shadow in her peripheral vision, and she kicked her right leg backward with her foot slamming into his stomach and knocking him to the ground. She continued to help Arica to her feet and then turned to a red-faced boiling angry Brock as he pulled himself from the hot pavement.

"You're gonna wish you never done that Jones."

She held out a hand as motioned him toward her, "Come on Turner. Come teach me a lesson."

Tessa had never fought Brock in the fighting ring; they studied different styles. He studied the brute strength techniques of brawling and wrestling where she studied martial arts requiring more finesse. As soon as he was on his feet, he charged Tessa nearly head first, and she smoothly moved from his path. His rage would make this fight even easier than she expected. He would act rashly and make rookie mistakes. Opportunities she could easily exploit. He swung at her with all his might, but Tessa was able to anticipate his movements. With the ferocity of his swings, he shifted his weight to add power to his punch every time. The downside for him was that she could see that punch coming from a mile away and she could dodge the blows effortlessly.

She let him swing at her a couple more times until she saw a few instructors headed their way to break apart the fight. She had a point to make, and she wanted Brock to understand, so she moved in to make that point. With his next swing, she caught his fist in her right hand, and rolled under his arm, twisting his arm awkwardly behind his back. Tessa pulled the arm back further, and he squealed in pain. She kicked the back side of his knees, and he fell to the ground, but she held onto the arm. With him in full submission she leaned forward to whisper in his ear, "I warned you to leave her alone."

Mr. Talbot, the science instructor, was now jogging to her, "Miss Jones, Miss Jones…" He was trying to get her attention, but she focused on Brock.

He laughed despite his pain, "I'm going to kill you."

Tessa was surprised that she didn't hesitate in her response, "Not if I kill you first." She brought her other arm down on his strained arm and heard the bone snap, and she let go. He grabbed his arm and turned around violently gazing hatefully at Tessa.

"Tessa, inside. I'll have to send a note to your parents." She turned to follow the instructor inside, but she saw that shadow behind her move again to strike.

She turned to see Brock lunging toward her this time with a knife in his uninjured hand. She reacted and with a fury of fists and a powerful roundhouse kick. Tessa backed him into the brick wall of the school building. She could see pure fear in his eyes as he was now weaponless and broken. He might have even regretted picking on Arica at that moment. She held her right foot to his throat and pushed him against the building making it hard for him to breath. She could hear Mr. Talbot screaming, but she couldn't make out the words. Tessa was consumed with anger and was blind to everything around her. She lowered her leg releasing him but planted a fist firmly in the wall next to his skull. What she wanted to do was crush that skull.

She stared intently into his eyes until it was clear that Tessa wasn't messing around and she meant business.

Brock Turner tucked tail and ran out of the schoolyard as fast as his legs could carry him. Tessa left behind a couple of cracked bricks where her fist had slammed into the wall. She didn't think she had hit the wall that hard. Mr. Talbot seemed equally confused by the broken blocks, but he quickly shifted his concern back to Tessa's disobedience.

Evie followed Tessa back inside the school where they sat outside the headmaster's office as Mr. Talbot dictated the letter home to her parents. It was a small price to pay for protecting her friend, and she didn't anticipate a lot of trouble when she got home. Brock had been sent home with these notes hundreds of times, and he was still in school; Tessa could survive this one. She watched as a group of teachers shuffled to the hallway and out the building to return a few minutes later in a hushed conversation.

Mr. Talbot handed Tessa her note and then sent the Jones girls on their way home. Tessa and Evie left the school to find her brother Andy waiting in the parking lot with the families rusted red pickup. Tessa helped Evie into the passenger seat.

"You guys are late."

"Yeah, sorry we got held up."

Evie was bursting to tell, "Tessa beat up Brock Turner."

"Thanks, Evie." Tessa sighed.

Andy raised an eyebrow at her, "Brock Turner, huh?" She paused waiting for the lecture, "Good job. That goon probably deserved it."

She grinned a little in surprise that her brother was proud of her action. She hoped her parents would feel the same, but nothing was that easy. Tessa was sure that some punishment would be in store. She climbed over the tailgate and sat down in the bed of the truck with her back against the cab and pulled her hood and scarf up to cover her face and her pair of goggles to protect her eyes from the dust. Tessa looked back at the cracked bricks on the school wall and noticed Mrs. Williams in the classroom window nearby. She looked at Tessa with a wary eye. Tessa had never seen Mrs. Williams look at her this way. She seemed to have a concerned look, one that Tessa didn't understand. She looked scared. But of what? There were always fights at school. Why did this time seem different?

The road home was a bumpy gravel road through the rural farming country. The ride was long enough to give Tessa plenty of time to think about everything that had transpired. She gazed out the back of the pickup truck watching the trail of dust billow out behind them. She wondered how long people could live like this under so much fear. Fear of Evos. Fear of death. She knew that with the dust and the dry weather the crops wouldn't sustain life forever. This world was dying, and they were all just struggling to exist until the end. The faults of previous generations had ruined the world and left them with nothing. Tessa's faith in humanity was nearly non-existent, but her defense of her friend gave her a sliver of hope. If just one person could stand up against a tyrant, then others could do so too. If everyone could have the courage to make a stand then maybe the human race stood a chance. If not, then what was the point of all this struggle? There had to be an end to the suffering. Where would it stop?

6

The truck pulled into the long dirt driveway and up to the old two-story farmhouse that Tessa and her family called home. Two empty rocking chairs on the porch swayed in the wind. The house itself had lost most of its color, but in the daylight, you could see a bit of the blue paint peeking through the grim. To the right and back behind the house was a metal pole barn which housed the family's farm equipment. It wasn't in much better shape than the house. Everything seemed to crumble in this hot, humid climate eventually.

Her friend Sam had beat them home and was leaning up against his dirt bike parked in the driveway, "I expected all home sooner."

Tessa jumped over the tailgate, "It's a long story."

Andy answered for her, "Brock Turner needed an attitude adjustment, and Tessa thought she was the one for the job."

"Nice," Sam agreed the bully got what he deserved.

Tessa clarified, "He was picking on Arica, and I had no intention of just watching. Sorry, I'll have to eat dinner and discuss this with my parents. Can you hang out for a few?"

"Sure, I can get a headstart on salvaging the Dust Devil spoils."

"That would be great. Thanks, Sam."

The three kids entered the house late for dinner. Tessa's fight with Brock had caused the delay, and she would have to explain that to her parents. Tessa's mother was hard at work in the kitchen cleaning up the dirty pots from dinner while waiting for her family to arrive at the table. She was a frail and sickly woman who continued to press forward. The years had been rough and time had not been kind to her, but she worked hard to provide for her family. She had fixed the same as most nights a meager pot roast with a few potatoes, noodles and some bread. Food was scarce, and this was a substantial meal although there was barely enough for everyone to have a decent portion.

They had to be careful and ration their food to save for the harsh winter months.

She handed her mother the note from the Dean and Andy left out the back door to call father to dinner. Tessa's mother pursed her chapped lips and tucked her short scraggly brown hair behind an ear. Her face looked rough like it had been weathered out in a dust storm and in truth that was part of the reason. Tessa's mother would have been pretty if the farm hadn't happened to her. This life had a way of weighing on a person and breaking them both mentally and physically. It had succeeded in diminishing her physical beauty, but her spirit remained brilliant. It was one of the bright spots in Tessa's life.

Her mother had overwhelming hope and inspiration, and that was what kept the family going most days, but some days it was harder than others for her to remain positive. The optimism was draining to maintain, and sometimes Tessa could hear her mother crying late at night when she thought no one was listening. But she would never show that weakness to any of her children, she remained a strong pillar; even though she was just as broken as everyone else inside, she never let it show.

Her father came in the back door with Andy as her mother was reading the note, "What's that?"

"A note from the school, Tessa was in a fight today," and answered.

"Fighting? That's not like you Tessa. What happened?"

Tessa knew her father would not take the news lightly. He was a stern and hardened man who had the pressure of providing for his family and meeting his quotas to keep the farm. The H.I.V.E required all farms to yield a certain amount of food to remain operational. Otherwise, they would move in someone else who could maintain the numbers. He sat at the table, face covered in dirt awaiting her answer.

"He was picking on one of the science kids, my friend Arica." She looked at him as he started to eat and he peered back at her wanting more information. The rest of the family ate in silence as Tessa answered her father's silent questions, "Brock Turner."

He stopped eating and put down his silverware, "Tessa, do you know what kind of problems a fight with Brock Turner can do to this family?"

She knew the possible consequences, but at the moment it was the right thing to do, no matter the consequence. Her father wouldn't see it her way. He had one job, to see that the family survived and the Turners were the best hunters in the area. Their family was the best at one thing, and that was killing. They supplied the community with game meat, and Tessa's family depended on that source of protein.

"I can hunt father." She offered a solution to the problem.

"I need you to work on the equipment, and you still have school. What time will there be for hunting?"

"I'll make time."

He sighed and returned to his food, "I'll have to talk to old Turner and see what I can do. Did he hurt you?"

Evie's innocent little voice delivered the final blow, "Tessa broke his arm."

Her father slammed down his hands on the table, "Damn it, Tessa. You go on out and work in the barn. No supper for you tonight. Maybe you'll learn how important food is and who you shouldn't mess with."

Tessa solemnly left the table and headed to the barn. She was a little grateful for her father's heated temper, at least she didn't have to listen to a long lecture. She just got yelled at instead, and that was quick. She deserved it. Tessa knew she shouldn't have done it, but if she could go back and do it again, she would have done the same thing. She accepted the fact that she would go the bed tonight hungry and it wasn't the first time; nor would it be the last. Hunger was inevitable in this life, whether it was her father's punishment or a lack of food.

Sam was waiting for Tessa in the barn while sorting through the equipment recovered from the Dust Devil attack. Unfortunately for them, the part that Sam needed was not among the salvaged parts. That meant they would need to visit the scrapyard, which left a sour taste in Tessa's mouth. The scrapyard was a dangerous spot and not a place she liked visiting. She would much rather get her parts from the town's weekend market, but there were some things that the market couldn't supply. Tessa and Sam filled their packs with parts and electronics they thought might be a fair trade for the right transmission he needed for the family farm truck.

They jumped on their dirt bikes and headed out away from town and toward the scrapyard. Some called it just the "Yard," and it was the territory of Static Shock. He was their local Evo overlord for lack of a better description. Most humans obeyed any Evos in their local area. It was just easier to comply. Static Shock controlled the area's access to materials, and he leveraged that in addition to his superhuman power to control static electricity. He had an entourage of human minions who did most of his bidding. The human traders aligned themselves with the most power in hopes to make a better life for themselves, but Evos couldn't care less about humans. All it took was one disappointment, and they faced elimination without a second thought. However, Static Shock was hardly ever seen since his humans did all the work for him. In all the trips Tessa had made to the Yard she had never met him, and she wasn't interested in that changing anytime soon. The goal was to get in and out without drawing any attention.

The two approached a rusted iron gate with an expansive heap of trash beyond. It was a twisted pile of old automobiles, tractors, airplanes, equipment, and electronics. It was a proverbial gold mine to anyone working in the agricultural district. A farm was only profitable if it could manage to maintain the equipment need to care for and harvest crops. The sun was still up, so the gates were still open, but there wasn't much daylight left. The Yard wasn't someplace you wanted to be after dark. The place attracted all of the wrong people once the sun went down. It wasn't the best place for two kids to be, so it was imperative that they search quickly and efficiently.

They entered the gates and past the armed guards, heading toward the section of the Yard with the automotive parts. Truck parts were hard to come by in the ag district, but not impossible to find. Static Shock sent his humans to the ruins of Oklahoma City to scavenge for new parts. It was essential to keep an inventory readily available to maintain that leverage over the area. Truck parts were a top priority for the scavengers.

Once Sam and Tessa reached their destination, they dismounted their bike and began searching through the piles. They stayed close to the bikes. If they were left unattended, they would be stolen or raided for parts. People here could be desperate and rude. Some are willing to do anything to get what they want, and that was part of why this place was so dangerous. You never know what a person might do if they were backed up against a wall. If they were desperate, then they were capable of almost anything. People notoriously disappear at the Yard never to be seen again. They go in, but they never come out.

As they were searching for a transmission, Tessa heard a voice she wished she hadn't, "Jones." It was a deep and gruff voice with an authoritative tone.

Tessa sighed and turned to face her challenger, "Turner."

Brock Turners older brother Angus loomed just feet away with two of his muscle-bound goons. "You got a set on you, to be out and about here after what you did to my brother."

"No offense but he deserved it."

"We're down a set of hands on the farm now that his arm is broken."

"Well tell him not to be an asshole, and maybe he won't break so many bones."

"I think we otta' return the favor. You got a sharp mouth girlie. I think someone should teach you a lesson."

"Are you gonna teach me?"

He picked up a tire iron from the junk pile, "I was planning on it."

Tessa couldn't resist, "I'm not sure your melon has the capacity to teach anyone anything."

"You think you're so smart. Let's see how tough you are."

Sam stepped forward, "You planning on talking all day? Or are we gonna do this?"

The three thugs rushed Tessa and Sam but they knew it was coming and it was easy to anticipate their brute force attack, so typical. Two of them went for Tessa since she was the primary target one of which was Angus. The other engaged Sam to keep him occupied and prevent him from helping Tessa. It didn't matter. Tessa could handle two. She reached behind her head to pull her batons sticking out of her backpack. She planted a foot in Angus' stomach as he charged her, sending him backward and to the ground. The other got a quick flurry of her batons to all his sensitive organs; kidneys, head, throat, and ribs. She finished him off by grabbing his head and slamming it down into her knee.

By that time, Angus was back up and ran his head into her stomach pushing her down to the ground and onto her back. His attempts to grapple her nearly succeeded, but she managed to wiggle out and return to her feet. He was angry now and not interested in fighting. He discovered he wasn't going to win as easily as he had hoped. Sam had defeated his combatant and Tessa was sure she had broken a few of his other friend's ribs.

Angus drew a pistol and pointed it at Tessa. Was he trying to scare her or was he planning on pulling the trigger? Tessa wasn't sure at that point. It was a point-blank shot, and if he took it, that would be her end. Sam began trying to get his attention by offering any number of items they had in their packs in exchange for Tessa's safety. Tessa just stared him in the eyes. She didn't want to blink for fear of missing the right moment.

Tessa waited for Angus to glance in Sam's direction and she grabbed his wrist holding the gun. Applying the correct amount of pressure at just the right point and his wrist buckled causing the weapon to point up and away from Tessa. She stepped toward him twisting the wrist and the gun further into an uncomfortable position. Pressing his wrist upward with his arm following suit she slid under the arm and turned. His body was forced to move with the arm and unless he wanted it to snap like his brothers. She rolled him over himself and removed the gun from his hand in the process. Tessa tumbled back to her feet and landed kneeling next to him with the gun now pointed at his temple.

The unexpected sound of slow clapping reverberated down the junk lined pathway. A figure walked toward them as he laughed and appeared amused by the spectacle he had just witnessed. "Bravo. You dear, are quite the little murderess." She saw a figure dressed in all black with spiky blond hair. He couldn't have been more than twenty or so years old.

Tessa lowered the gun and stood to face him. She knew deep down in the churning pit of her stomach who this was. Tessa was face to face with Static Shock and an entourage of human lackeys. She cleared her throat and swallowed hard trying to keep her cool, "Sorry for the commotion. I meant no harm. Just defending myself."

"I'd say." He had a sense of amusement in his voice. "It seems that you are more than capable of defending yourself. I could use talent like yours on my team."

She had to tread lightly, "With great respect, I have little time for a side job. I come from a family of

83

poor humble farmers, and they need me to protect our lands. We supply food to this area. Including payment to you."

He paused in thought, "But I like you. You have spirit. Are you sure you aren't interested in a new career? I could offer far more than H.I.V.E."

"I believe you could, but my family needs me."

"I can see why." He waved his hands, and his loyal humans picked Angus and his friend up from the ground and had them escorted from the Yard. "See that you don't come back. You should never have attacked my precious…" He turned to her for a name.

"Tessa."

"There now they won't bother you here ever again and neither will anyone else for that matter. If you should change your mind, you know where I'll be. I'll keep a spot open for you."

"Thank you for your hospitality."

"Now what brings you to the Yard?"

"We were searching for a truck transmission."

He paused to look at his remaining entourage and stomped his foot, "Don't just stand there! Find my Tessa what she seeks!"

The men scrambled all over each other and the junk piles, searching for the truck transmission. After a few minutes of loud clanking and shouting voices one human presented the transmission to Static Shock. He motioned for Tessa to retrieve the part and she removed her pack to present her payment. He waved a hand, "No payment. Just consider my proposition."

He turned to leave, and Tessa could hear Sam exhale. That was a dangerous encounter, and they were lucky to have escaped with their lives. It could have easily gone another way. Had he been in a bad mood he could have been angered by the fight on his turf, and that could have been a death sentence for Tessa, Sam, Angus and his friends. Instead, it had gone in her favor, striking another blow to the Turner family. They might as well forget about mending any ties with that family. Tessa had broken both boys and gotten them banned from the Yard. She doubted her father would be successful in repairing that relationship.

Sam and Tessa returned to the farm, and from there Sam headed home to start working on installing the new transmission. Tessa had offered to help with the repair. She didn't want to have to face her family and tell them about what just happened. Sam told her if he had any problems he would let her know and then reminded her that she had her own repairs to tend. So she stayed home and returned to the barn. She would tell her family the story later. More than likely they would hear it through the gossip mill. It wouldn't take long for them to find out. It was a small community and news spread like wildfire.

She enjoyed having the barn to herself where she could hear herself think and work with her hands. Tessa's job on the farm was to keep the machinery in working order. Her family was aware of her engineering talent that she hid away when she was at school. Without her at home, they would have to hire a mechanic, and they didn't have much to barter. Having Tessa around meant they had more money to buy food and other necessities, but it looked like they would be saving more by not buying game meat as well. She figured her father would eventually barter a deal with the elder Turner and once everything boiled over, they would be able to get meat again. For now, they would make do without and Tessa could find some time to hunt in the meantime.

The first thing Tessa did when she got inside the barn was to turn on the radio she set up next to her workbench in the corner. There was never any new music, but at least some people still had copies of the old stuff. There were always people out there that would broadcast their music collection over the radio waves, and Tessa had rigged up a device to receive the signals. The radio pirates were enemies of the H.I.V.E, but the government didn't have the workforce or resources to shut them all down. The H.I.V.E liked their propaganda, and sometimes the air jockeys wanted to speak their opinion on particular political agendas. The H.I.V.E didn't much care for opinions. They wanted everyone to believe in one thing; the H.I.V.E mission. Every once and awhile someone would cross the line, and Tessa assumed the government shut them down because the frequency would turn to dark empty static.

She cranked up the volume to her favorite station which played what the jockey called rock. Seemed like a silly name for a type of music but she liked it anyway. The song "Welcome to the Jungle" by a band called Guns and Roses was playing, and with equally outrageous names to their genre Tessa jammed out to the catchy tune. She headed over toward the tractor and climbed up the steep ladder and into the cab. She cranked the key, and the engine turned over. She sighed in relief that the problem wasn't an engine issue. Her father worked this machine far too hard if he wasn't careful, one day Tessa wouldn't be able to fix it.

She turned off the engine and climbed from cab singing away as loud as she could. She grabbed a wrench from her workbench and sang into one end of it acting like a complete fool. She could let loose here in the barn. The family was inside, and it was too late to run equipment in the field. No one would bother her at this time of night. This hour was her usual alone time, and she enjoyed it very much.

She took her remaining time to give the machine a good look over. She tightened bolts here or there, checked hoses, and greased what needed to be. Regular maintenance was essential to being a prosperous farmer, and the family was glad to have Tessa's capable hands here to maintain all their equipment.

As she worked, she continued to sing along to the sounds of rock on the radio, until the music cut off and an excited broadcast personality took over the frequency. "We interrupt this broadcast to announce that Kansas City has fallen to Evo control. The fighting began early this morning and lasted throughout the day. General Landon and his troops fought valiantly to wipe this scourge from…." There was static, and the propaganda announcer was faded out, and a new voice emerged. Tessa rolled out from under the tractor and sat up wiping grease from her hands with a towel and listening intently to voice from the radio. "It's lies, all lies they tell you. They want you to believe that Evos are evil and what is wrong with this world, but they created us, and now they only want to silence us. They were fine when we were out doing their dirty work, but once we figured out what they were up to there was no other option but action. There are Evos who are out for domination, but there are those of us who want to do what's right for this world and we…" There was static again, and the radio was silent. Tessa walked over and stood in front of the receiver waiting to hear another voice, but it never came. The H.I.V.E must have pulled the feed. Kansas City was close. Too close.

Tessa jumped as the door to the barn opened, but it wasn't anyone she expected who walked through. The engineering instructor, Professor Green, strolled into the barn, "Sorry to startle you, Tessa." He walked toward her, his crazed brown hair bouncing as he walked and his thick glasses nearly falling off his nose. It was strange to see him in anything other than his lab coat, but here he was in plain clothes in the middle of her barn.

"What are you doing here?" No other instructor had ever visited her at home.

"I wanted to talk to you about school. I did not tell the Dean I was visiting you at home. That's between the two of us and your parents. I already took the liberty of speaking with them first." He sat down on a wooden stool next to her workbench and started admiring her tools.

"What did you talk to them about?"

"Your performance at school and I'm not talking about your little tussle today."

"There's nothing wrong with my school work."

"Precisely!" He pointed at her matter of factly, "Tessa you are surprisingly mediocre at every subject in school. Not terrible but not quite good enough to be placed in a different work capacity. But I've noticed that you are far more intelligent than you lead on." This realization wasn't good; she couldn't let him know she was trying to alter her destiny by throwing her test scores. She remained silent. "Not only have I noticed your intelligence but you have a knack for combat as well. You are what I call the perfect well-rounded student. You could work in any capacity. You could choose your destiny."

"I have a destiny, and its here." She went back to work trying to ignore his presence.

"Do you want to be stuck out here on this farm for the rest of your life? You could do so much more for yourself."

"My family is here."

"With higher status comes added perks. You could send food or aid from the H.I.V.E here to your family."

She wasn't going to be tempted by his attempts. He had no proof of his claims, "I think you're mistaken and you should leave."

He put his hands up in surrender, "I'm only offering solutions Tessa, you can't hide forever, and eventually someone else will figure you out. Your display today has brought a lot of attention your way, and you'll have to answer their questions sometime."

He left her to her work where she could ponder what her next move would be. Tessa knew he was right and after today people would be watching her. Brock was a top combat student, and he ranked at the top because he's rarely beaten and she made beating him look like child's play. She would have to be very careful tomorrow at school and in the future. Maybe if she kept her head down, this whole incident would blow over, and everyone would forget. For now, she needed to try to keep a low profile.

She cleaned up her work area and turned off the still silent radio. She was preoccupied with her problems, but she was still concerned about Kansas City falling into Evo hands. Tessa seemed to worry constantly even though these things were out of her control. She returned to the house wrapped up in her thoughts. Her mother was doing dishes in the kitchen when she came in the back door.

Tessa sat down at the kitchen table knowing her mother surely had something to say. She stopped washing dishes and looked around the corner toward the living room. There were no sounds of movement, so she pulled a plate from a cabinet where she had hidden a bit of food for Tessa. She set the plate in front of her, "Hurry up and eat before your father catches me." Tessa started shoveling in the food, and her mom sat down across from her. "You know you don't have to stay here Tessa. We can manage without you."

"Mom, Professor Green is wrong. I'm just not as good at those things as he thinks I am. Maybe he's hoping to promote a student to engineering. We haven't had anyone qualify for a while."

Her mom could always tell when she was lying, "Tessa, I know you have a knack for engineering. You realize you do work on the farm equipment around here and you've made repairs in the house here for me. If you are destined for greater things then so be it."

"I'm not leaving."

"Well, I didn't know you were good at fighting. I would rather you go into engineering than go off to war."

"I'm not going anywhere, mom."

She finished eating, and her mom reached out to grab her hands holding them tight, "You have a chance to make a real difference in this world, and that makes me proud. Don't stay here and waste your talent."

Tessa pulled her hands away, "I don't have any talent. It's all just a misunderstanding."

She left the kitchen and went upstairs to her bedroom where she could be alone again. She put on a comfy pair of pajamas and laid down to bed staring up at the dark ceiling. She couldn't sleep with all the thoughts swirling in her head. She wondered what that voice on the radio meant about not all Evos being bad. All of them that she had ever known had done nothing but cause trouble, and the ones the H.I.V.E reported on were responsible for so much death and destruction. How could they be good? The power went to their heads, and that's why the H.I.V.E collects up all the Evos. She wondered what happened to them once collected. She had to admit that the H.I.V.E's operations were sketchy and she didn't fully believe all of the propaganda, but she couldn't side with the Evos either. All she wanted to do was survive them both and live out her life here with her family. She eventually floated off into dreams which weren't much better than reality. There was no escaping the fears of reality even in the subconscious mind.

7

Tessa reluctantly returned to school the next day. She knew that the gossip would spread through the school like wildfire. She could feel eyes following her down the hall; judging her every move. Tessa had always felt out of place, but this feeling was even worse. Their eyes weighed heavy, and she felt trapped under a microscope. It was in her best interest to keep her head down and voice quiet. Hopefully, this would pass, and she could return to her normal feeling of oddity.

Even Arica and Sam wanted to keep their distance from her. Arica did offer a quiet thank you despite the watchful eyes. She couldn't blame them for steering clear. If Tessa were in their shoes, she would do the same. Testing was just weeks away, and all she needed to do was play it cool until then. After placement, she wouldn't have to attend school any longer, and she could leave all of this in her past.

It was a lonely day with little to no interaction, shunned by her classmates. Brock had returned to school with his arm in a cast and a pair of angry eyes that burned through her like lasers. She was sure he wished for a quick recovery so he could settle the score with her. Part of her hoped for the same. Tessa would do the same as she had yesterday leaving him beaten and embarrassed. He deserved everything he got from her and then some.

For the first half of the day, Tessa managed to stay out of the limelight and tucked away in a corner. After lunch, the day began to change drastically, but it had absolutely nothing to do with her. During chemistry lecture, the skies outside turned eerily dark. Large thunder clouds billowed in fast and unrelenting. They moved too fast to be natural, and that only meant one thing, Evos. The students slowly turned their attention from class to the ominous clouds. As the students began to congregate around the windows, the instructors started to panic.

They all turned to their walkies to discuss what action to take if any. For now, it seemed calm but all that could change at any moment. Tessa tried to think of what Evos could be responsible for the disruption. There were several known Evos who had made names for themselves. Learning about the important ones were part of their studies. The lessons were more about what to watch out for and how to avoid them. No one would ever dream of engaging an Evo in combat. That fight would only end in one way; six feet under.

Tessa got her answer when a petite woman dropped out of the clouds and hovered in the air surrounded by the swirling storm clouds. She was far away but not so distant that Tessa couldn't make out the distinguishing long silver hair that indicated that this Evo was Gale Force. She was a weather manipulating Evo with close ties to the Evo's resistance movement. That was the same group that overtook Kansas City, which Tessa had heard about the previous evening on the radio. The radio had not indicated that the resistance was moving further to the west of Kansas City, but Tessa could venture to guess that Gale Force was here to scout ahead.

There was a flash of light which could be traced from ground to air and struck the floating Evo provoking her to stir the clouds for an attack. The winds picked up quickly to hurricane-like speeds, and the instructors sounded evacuation alarms and started herding students to the old bomb shelter beneath the school, not that they would be safe there if an Evo wanted in bad enough. They practiced these drills often, and it wasn't the first time the instructors raised the alarms for an actual emergency.

Evos moved in and out of these outlying farm communities claiming them as territory. Right now this particular area had been declared by Static Shock who was no doubt responsible for the attack on Gale Force. She was invading his territory, and he wasn't going to give it up without a fight. Tessa was glued to Gale Force and watched as Static Shock floated up toward her as they prepared to go toe to toe. An in-flight battle was something Tessa had not seen before, and it seemed like something exciting to watch, so she lingered in the class as everyone scurried to shelter.

Arica found Tessa and tugged at her arm to pull her toward safety, and she reluctantly complied. They all shuffled into the bomb shelter as the storm raged above with sounds of debris wildly whipping about and the sound of shockwaves thundering across the sky. The air boomed, and the ground shook as these titans batted above. Tessa couldn't help but wonder if there would be anything left by the time they were through.

Tessa searched the shelter for Evie and the more she sought, the more concerned she grew. She couldn't find her sister and Evie's instructor had no idea where she was. One of the smaller children tugged on her shirt to tell her that Evie had gone to the restroom just before the alarm sounded. Tessa feared that her sister was upstairs huddled in the middle of this war zone. Tessa approached the Dean at the shelter door and pleaded with him to let her retrieve Evie from upstairs, but he would not allow it.

Tessa informed Arica and Sam that she couldn't sit around and wait for her sister to die. She had to take action, and they agreed to have her back. Tessa and Sam distracted the Dean while Arica opened a back door to the shelter. The three of them poured out the door as instructors scrambled to prevent them from leaving. The instructors refused to exit the refuge after them, and instead, they sealed the door leaving the trio to their demise.

"Thanks for helping. You can stay here if you like." Tessa was grateful for such friends but didn't want to see them get hurt.

Sam poised for action as usual, "And let you have all the fun?"

"I wouldn't call it fun." Arica was a little out of her element, but she would stay close to Tessa and Sam for protection. "Let's just try not to die."

"First thing first; weapons." Sam knew that the training hall was on the way to the younger children's wing.

Arica wasn't planning on fighting, but she did want protection, "And shields please."

They made their way to the training floor and suited up with body armor and weapons. Tessa strapped a pair of side arm handguns to her thighs and a couple of metal batons to her back. Sam chose a pair of handguns as well as an assault rifle. Arica just suited up with some armor and distributed comms to the group and an infrared scanner to track heat signatures. She hoped it would come in handy locating Evie. Arica helped the other two fill mags and stock up.

As they were gearing up a booming crash echoed through the practice gym as the ceiling opened up and something or someone came hurtling toward the gym floor. The equipment lockers were a balcony level above the gym practice floor, and the three peered down from their concealment to see what had fallen through the gaping hole now in the ceiling. The rubble now scattered across the floor moved, and they could hear a faint groan as Static Shock emerged and stumbled to his feet. Arica looked down at the infrared scanner and a look a panic fell on her face. She pointed to the gym doors below as Tessa saw Evie come into view. Her innocent child figure hesitated in curiosity as she tried to see what caused all the commotion.

Tessa wasted no time in making her final preparations. She refused to stand by and watch her sister face an Evo alone. Tessa opened the programming panel on the left arm bracer and input the parameter for her suit. She closed the panel and pressed the button in the center of her chest, and her armor hummed faintly as it powered up. Tessa programmed her suit to absorb as much electrically charged energy as it could. Hopefully, it would be enough that she could survive any of Static Shock's powered attacks. The wired piping running throughout the suit glowed an electric blue indicating it was ready for battle. She pulled her goggles over her head and eyes. She had engineered theses goggle especially to give combat readouts, and Tessa needed every tactical advantage she could get. Her two friends tried to convince her to change her mind silently, but Tessa only saw one choice.

She peered down into the gym as Static Shock noticed his young guest and he started to move toward Evie. Evie froze in fear as the Evo monster approached her with a glower on his face. Tessa moved quickly toward the balcony railing and launched herself up over the rail falling to the gym floor below. The movement drew Static Shock's attention, but he watched in curiosity as she approached. It wasn't often that a human would challenge an Evo and he was amused. She vaulted over rubble and slid down a table with a broken leg which slanted at an angle placing her squarely between Static Shock and Evie. After the slide, her feet met the ground, and she rolled over her right shoulder forward into position pulling the batons from her back in one seamless string of motion. She was now crouched in attack position facing Static Shock and blocking him from Evie.

She slowly stood tall in front of the Evo and nodded Evie to find cover. Tears filled the child's eyes as she ran to hide behind some nearby debris. Tessa figured Evie would witness her sister's death, but Tessa only needed to survive long enough; hopefully, Gale Force would come to finish him off.

Static Shock smirked at her and rubbed his palms together creating flickering sparks to creep across his skin. "I see why you declined the job. Working for the resistance?" He was charging up his energy, so Tessa activated her batons, which she set to emit positive charges hoping to render his attacks useless. "Doing a little recon work for your masters last night?"

He flung an outstretched hand hurling a negative charge toward her. She rolled to the right to avoid contact. The charge landed behind her crashing into the wall causing more destruction. She seized the moment to bridge the space between them. He could throw charges all day, but she was hoping that was the extent of his abilities. She was figuring that his melee skills were lacking and she preferred the close game. Hoping her combat skills were better than his, she moved into close quarters combat. On the other hand, it also made her closer to strike with direct energy blasts. She hoped the suit held up under the electrical strain.

He tried to stop her with an electric attack to her midsection, but the suit neutralized the negative charge. All she needed to do was absorb was the physical impact which was also reduced by the armor's padding. She knocked his arm away and with an elbow landed a hit to his jaw and then a counter blow with the left baton to his right midsection. She aimed her blow as hard as she could with all her might at his kidneys to magnify the destructive force of the hit. She focused on pinpoint attacks. Every hit had to count. She could not allow him to gain the upper hand.

He staggered back, and from the corner of Tessa's eye she saw Gale Force float in from the hole in the ceiling, but she did not rush in to finish her enemy. Instead, she perched on the second-floor balcony adjacent to her friends. Sam had surely noticed her arrival, and she was undoubtedly in the crosshairs of his assault rifle. Tessa would let Sam watch Gale Force so she could focus on Static Shock.

He moved in again hastily which opened him up for an easy hit. Two precision hits with each baton one to the left collarbone and the other to the right side of the skull followed by a roundhouse to the face. He stumbled back regaining his composure, and then he charged. Tessa tried to spin out of the way, but he moved inhumanly fast and grappled her to the ground. His hands gripped tightly around her neck, and he let his energy surge. The suit did not protect Tessa's neck as the negative energy flowed through her body in excruciating pain.

Tessa pushed through the pain and flung Static Shock over her head with feet planted firmly in his chest she managed to toss him quite a distance. Tessa sprung back to her feet with batons at the ready. He started throwing wave after wave of negative energy bolts at her in a frantic attempt to stay out of her striking range. He threw bolts at hanging debris in hopes of burying her in the rubble. She realized something. He was scared of her. True, he was a lower level Evo, but she never expected to win this fight.

She moved in again with more aggression and with a new found confidence, and they collided in a barrage of hits and misses. She was landing more hits than he was and she was focused intently on her enemy. Rage started to well up inside her; she could end this Evo. He had threatened their town for the last few years raiding supplies and hurting citizens and here she was poised to remove him from his position of power. He wasn't as dominant as she had thought. A simple human could best him. She wondered if there were more Evos that could be challenged by ordinary folk.

As she continued the onslaught of melee, she shoved Static Shock up against a wall, and she could see he was at his end. From her peripheral vision, she noticed Gale Force in her dark purple suit and silver hair streaked with matching purple approached slowly with arms up offering peace, "Welcome sister." She smiled, and Tessa was confused.

Tessa looked down to see that her hands were pulsing with a pinkish purple glow around them and Static Shock engulfed in a similar light. Her left hand outstretched toward him, and he was paralyzed unable to move. In a panic, Tessa drew the sidearm from her right holster and fired three shots into Static Shock. He slid down the wall and expired on the floor, and there was no more strange glow.

Tessa returned her attention to Gale Force as she clapped her hands together in congratulations, "Perfect. How long have you had your powers?"

Tessa began to tremble with fear, and she dropped her weapons; staring at her hands in horror. She was not able to process what had just happened, "That was you." Tessa pointed to Gale Force.

"I'm afraid not. My powers are not even close to yours, and I think you already know that. Is this the first time?" She tried to move toward Tessa.

Tessa backed away repulsed, "It can't be me."

"Well, it was someone. Don't be frightened there is help for people like us."

Tessa pointed in anger at Gale Force, "No! I'm nothing like you. You're a murderer."

Gale Force glanced at Static Shock's corpse, "And you're not?"

"I did what I had to."

"Yes, he would have killed you. Kill or be killed. But what will the humans do with you once they discover your secret."

"There's nothing to discover."

Gale Force was coy with her, "That's right keep telling yourself that. When you figure it out," she tossed a communicator earpiece to Tessa who let it drop in fear, "Call me. I'm willing to help. You got some pretty impressive power."

Gale Force flew away through the hole in the roof, and Tessa picked up the comm from the ground and shoved it in her pocket. She didn't want it falling into the wrong hands. Tessa had no intentions of calling Gale Force, but she had witnessed Tessa's secret and she couldn't risk anyone else finding out. She already had Arica, Sam and Evie to worry about and she needed to control the situation as much as possible. Her friends and sister came out of hiding, and they looked at her with awe. Or was it fear. She convinced them she was still the same Tessa but something changed. They looked at her differently now.

8

Tessa frantically rummaged through the wreckage of the combat room to find a first aid kit as Sam, Arica, and Evie watched in bewilderment. Tessa was in trouble, and her first instinct was to survive this tragedy. If she could make it through the rest of the day, perhaps she could buy herself enough time to figure out a master plan. Tessa needed to hurry before the H.I.V.E response team showed up to analyze the crime scene. Once she located the first aid kit, she found a needle and a tourniquet. She trusted the material into Arica's hands.

"What do you want me to do with this?" Arica was nervous and apprehensive about taking the kit.

"I need you to take a blood sample. You can analyze my blood, and we can figure out what's going on with me and fix it."

"Fix it? There's no way to fix it, Tessa."

Tessa hectically tried to explain, "I know, but you're smart maybe we can find a way to mask it temporarily. At least until I can figure out what to do." She paused to breathe for a moment running her hands through her hair as tears started to well up in her eyes. The stress was overwhelming and surreal. "I have no idea what to do, but I know I need your help. Please don't make me do this alone. Don't leave me now when I need you the most." She turned to address the other two, "I need all of you to help." She crouched down in front of Evie, "I know this is hard to understand but you have to keep this a secret between just us. If people find out about this, they will take me away forever. You will never see me again. Do you understand?" Wide-eyed little Evie nodded her head in comprehension.

Arica agreed to help with a worried look in her eye, "I'm not sure what you expect me to do with this."

"If nothing else, we can test for abilities so I know what to expect. I have to hide this, and there can't be any surprises."

Sam reminded her of the dangers she was facing. "We test at the end of the school year." His timeline wasn't helping Tessa's stress level at all.

Arica started to draw a vile of her blood, and she flinched momentarily, "Do you not think that has crossed my mind? I'm terrified, but I have to make it through this situation before I can even consider making it until the end of the school year. If I can't make it through today without anyone finding out, then I don't have a future at all and testing doesn't even matter." Arica finished up, and Tessa pulled down her sleeve, "We need to have the same story. Keep it simple. Gail Force did this; she killed Static Shock. All we did was find Evie and hid here out of sight." She wiped her prints from the gun that she used to kill Static Shock and tossed it into the surrounding debris. Tessa had worn the combat suit with gloves so fingerprints should not be an issue but she didn't want to take a chance of any trace DNA.

Sam looked up at the ceiling in the corner of the room, and Tessa followed his gaze to a camera. Tessa threw a piece of debris at the camera shattering it to pieces. It was the only one in the room, but it had recorded everything. She looked to Sam for help, "Take care of it." He nodded and sprinted off to make sure the footage disappeared. She wasn't sure they would be able to pull this off, but there was little choice. She could hear the response team vehicles pull into the gravel schoolyard and the sound of boots in the hallway became louder and louder until what she feared was upon her.

The militarized response team swooped in and secured the area immediately and that including sequestering their four eye-witnesses. The rest of the school emerged from the shelter, and the higher ranking teachers joined the response team in sorting out the crimes scene and assessing the damage. Mr. Talbot the headmaster agreed to cooperate and give the team full access to everything they needed. Professor Green lent his scientific expertise to the forensic investigators. The investigative team immediately separated the four witnesses for interrogation.

Tessa waited for what seemed like an eternity in one of the teacher's offices until a middle-aged blond woman in glasses entered the room holding manila file folders. She didn't even look up from the pages in the file to glance at Tessa. When she finally did, she sighed and closed the envelope, "Please have a seat," Tessa obeyed.

"Well, Tessa you've had quite an exciting day today haven't you?" She sat in another chair directly facing her. "What made you leave the shelter? Seems like a rash choice."

Tessa began to speak, but her throat felt raspy, and she cleared her throat, "My sister. She wasn't in the shelter."

"Bold move, taking it upon yourself to go after her, but at least you weren't alone. Lucky to have such loyal friends."

Tessa feigned a smile, "They are good friends."

"Hard to find these days." She paused to return to her line of questioning after her attempt to break the conversational ice. "And you came to the combat training room first before retrieving your sister?"

"Yes."

"Why?"

Tessa had thought it was apparent, but she humored her interrogator, "There were Evos, and I had no wish to run into either of them unarmed and without armor."

"Smart. We look for bold and savvy candidates like you for our team."

Being recruited for their team was the last thing Tessa wanted or any other military operation for that matter, so she needed to proceed with caution to avoid that classification. "I did what anyone would have done."

"Perhaps." She moved forward and removed the armor suit's operational wrist cuff and examined the settings, "Surprising..." she opened the file folder to write down a few notes. "You programmed them to negate Static Shock's power. What about Gail Force? What if you would have run into her?"

Tessa shrugged and continued her lie, "I guess I figured she would be flying and I would be more likely to run into Static Shock."

"Tell me what happened." This woman was like ice and Tessa couldn't tell if she believed any of Tessa's story.

"I saw Gail Force and Static Shock crash through the ceiling, and they fought in the combat room. Gail Force killed Static Shock."

She studied Tessa closely, "With a gun? Why would Gail Force use a gun?" The woman was skeptical of the story.

"I don't know why she did what she did. All I know is that she shot him and killed him."

She continued with an ongoing barrage of questions and Tessa couldn't help but wonder how the others were managing. She hadn't realized how many holes were in their story. She wasn't sure if this woman believed anything she was saying, but she had to continue with the lies. If they suspected anything, they might test her now rather than later, and that would be the end-game for Tessa. She tried her best to remain calm and composed on the outside, but on the inside, she was on the verge of losing her mind.

After the questioning was complete, she was allowed to leave and walked out into the combat room where the team continued collecting samples. They had found the gun and were currently running tests on it. She saw Professor Green with Static Shock's body. He was swabbing the body for any residue that they could analyze in a lab. She wasn't sure what they might find and if she would escape discovery but she had to remain optimistic.

She met up with Arica and Sam in the cafeteria where they had assembled all the other students. Their group had a corner all to their own because it seemed that not a single student wanted anything to do with any of them. After yesterday's fight and now this escapade, they looked at Tessa and her friends as troublemakers, and she couldn't blame them for thinking that way. If she could distance herself from herself right now, that would be what she would do, but instead, she remained trapped in her skin.

The H.I.V.E eventually dismissed Tessa and her friends, so she was optimistic that the ruse had worked, but deep down in the pit of her stomach, she remained pessimistic. These people were highly trained and skilled at their jobs. Surely they would see right through her. The suspense of not knowing was killing her slowly from the inside out.

She made arrangements with Arica to meet back at the school late night after dark to runs some preliminary tests on her blood sample. After the H.I.V.E team concluded their initial investigation, they dismissed school and sent all the students home. There was far too much destruction to the school to continue with the day, and there had been far too much excitement as well. It was best that everyone return home for the remainder of the day and start fresh tomorrow. That gave Tessa a little extra time to concoct some basic framework of a plan.

She met Evie outside the school, and they waited for Andy to pick them up. Evie just kept staring at her awkwardly, and once enough students had left, and there was no one within earshot she addressed the child, "What?"

"Are you a monster?"

"No! I'm just Tessa; your sister." She paused to wonder if she was becoming a monster.

"Teacher says Evos are monsters."

"Do you think I'm a monster?" Evie shook her head no, but it was all difficult for her to comprehend. "Look I haven't changed. I'm still the same as I was this morning and the day before that. Things have just become more complicated, and I need to time to figure out what to do. Can you hold on until I figure it out?"

"Yes. I don't want them to take you away."

"I don't want to go away either." She hugged her sister, "I promise I will do all that I can to stay, but you have to help me do that and keep this quiet. You can't tell anyone, including mom, dad, and Andy."

Evie made the motion as if she was zipping her lips and smiled back at her older sister in adoration. Evie looked up to her older sister for strength and right now Tessa felt like a leaf shaking in the wind. Tessa had always been able to get herself out of a tight spot, but this spot was suffocating. She hoped she could come through for Evie and be the role model she deserved. Tessa's whole family needed her, and she needed them just as much. The idea of being swept away to some unknown destination was terrifying, and it seemed impossible to quell her nerves, but she fought hard to remain positive and composed on the outside. She didn't want to scare Evie any more than she already had.

Once they were picked up and returned home, Tessa made sure that she kept family time brief and quickly retreated to the barn. Her workshop was the one place where mostly everyone left her alone. They knew that when she was working and focused on the task at hand peace and quiet helped her to finish successfully. Therefore Tessa got the personal space necessary to complete her work on time and correctly. She tinkered around on some farm equipment but didn't manage to get anything notable done. Tessa was far too distracted to accomplish anything at the moment. She was biding her time on pins and needles until she could meet up with Arica and have at least a few answers to a small portion of the questions that were swirling around in her head. There were so many questions swirling around in there and spawning new ones every second that Tessa half expected her head to rattle out loud to indicate maximum capacity. She could not quiet her thoughts and tonight's research endeavor was more likely to raise more questions than what they could answer.

Tessa returned to the house as late to avoid as much conversation as she could. She still got asked a few questions surrounding the commotion at school, but she managed to deflect the details. She refrained from telling them about her interview as a witness and that she had put her life in danger by leaving the shelter. They would eventually find out, but she would deal with that backlash when the time came. Right now that worry was but a drop in the bucket compared to the other problems she had to solve.

She finally slipped into bed and laid there awake staring at the ceiling wondering if this would be the last time she would sleep under this roof with her family. H.I.V.E could come and haul her away at any moment. She would disappear like a thief in the night, and no one would ever question it or hear from her again. She listened to the sounds from downstairs in the living room. Her father was listening to the radio getting his fill of what he called news. Tessa called it government propaganda because that was what it was. The loose collection of government holding on to the thread of power they had remaining was filling the minds of the remaining survivors with notions of hope and the promise of coming prosperity. There was nothing good happening in this world; it was dying, and humans would all destroy each other eventually. It was just a ticking time bomb waiting to explode.

Tessa waited until nearly an hour after she heard the last person stirring in the house before she moved from her bedroom. She quietly slid her bedroom window opened and slipped out and down the side of the house, using a trellis for a ladder. It wasn't the first time she had snuck out, and it didn't seem it would be the last. Not until she could figure out what was going on with her own body. She couldn't risk anyone else discovering her secret. She tiptoed to the barn although there was nothing that could hear her and blow her cover. The nights were eerie silent since the collapse, especially this far out in the country. So many animals had been wiped off the planet over the last few years, she knew the human race was on that extinction list but what wasn't clear how long they would last.

She rolled her dirt bike from the barn and started pushing it down the road. She didn't dare start the engine until she was far enough down the road that no one could hear. Once she was out of earshot, she kick-started the engine and headed back into town. The night was dark save for the moonlight that barely lit the road. She could see well enough without her headlight, and so she opted to leave it off. There were other farms to ride past, and it was best for her not to draw unwanted attention of any kind. She couldn't risk someone following and putting together the pieces. Plus bandits prayed on unarmed travelers more so at night, and so many of the roads remained deserted after dark, so it was unlikely she would meet anyone other than a bandit along the way at this time of the evening. After her recent self-discovery, she felt a twinge of pity for any fool who tried to stop her from reaching her destination on this night.

She pulled into the school's parking lot without incident and pulled her bike up to the stone building behind some bushes to conceal her presence. She found Arica and Sam waiting for her at the back entrance. They had tried to pick the lock and were unsuccessful. Tessa gripped the handle tight and snapped it off. The other two looked at her with worried expressions, but she only shrugged. Tessa had these abilities and might as well put them to use until she could figure out what to do with them. Besides, they needed access to the school, and she was desperate for the answers they might discover using the tools that the school provided. She made sure to cover their tracks and ensure that no one could tie them to the break-in.

The group made their way to the lab where Arica started processing Tessa's blood from earlier. She removed the test tube from the lab fridge and started running it through DNA analysis. The school taught courses to science aptitude students on how to recognize and decode Evo DNA. It was only an introductory course, but at least Arica had some knowledge of what markers might be suspect. While she was processing data, Sam decided to conduct some testing of this own. Tessa found herself in the destroyed combat room analyzing the force of her punch to determine the extent of her strength. Sam had her hit a wired monitoring punching bag to gauge the force of her strike. Sam was amazed to discover that her attack registered well above any other documented strength powered Evo.

He tried to convince her to spar with him to coax any other abilities out. It was a widespread belief that stress often triggered Evo abilities to surface, especially during a combat situation. The theory was that the mind was so focused on the fight that the super-human ability frequently appeared without notice as a subconscious response to the circumstances. Tessa wasn't willing to use one of her best friends as a test dummy on skills she had no idea what they might be or how to control them. Her experience with Static Shock had proved that combat could cause abilities to surface and she knew she had at least two abilities. She knew she had increased strength and whatever the glowing purple power was.

Arica's test only revealed more details about what they already knew. She pointed out the DNA markers to Tessa, "I can see that you have several abnormalities in your DNA sequence."

"How many?"

"It's hard to say exactly. Your sequence is extremely complex."

"Humor me. Ballpark?"

"More than I've ever seen." Arica hesitated, "More than I've ever heard of."

"What does that mean?" Tessa ran her fingers through her hair squeezing her head in frustrations.

"You have more anomalies than any other Evo record. Or at least to my knowledge."

"Are there any that you recognize?"

"A few, the strength of course, and there's another physical ability there, but I can't quite decipher it. There are quite a few mental abilities there as well."

"Mental abilities?" They were considered the most dangerous of Evo abilities. Mental abilities had the potential to drive an Evo mad, and mentally unstable Evos with that type of power could be hazardous.

"They're strong Tessa."

"What level?"

"Alpha."

Tessa sat down in the nearest chair, and both friends stared at her awaiting a response, but she did not react to that news. The overwhelming weight of the discovery made her numb. How could her mental abilities be a level alpha? That made her the highest class level in Evo mental abilities. "Do you know what kind of mental ability it is?"

"I can't tell by the DNA testing, but I can run some neural scans and see if I can learn more."

"Do whatever it takes."

Arica hooked a mess of electrodes up to her head and ran a series of neurological tests on her higher brain function. She worked long into the night, and everyone was getting tired, but they weren't getting any answers. The final results of the test were inconclusive, and the only morsel of information Arica could give her was that the power was a psionic power, but she couldn't tell much more than that. Psionic powers could be any number of powers like psychokinesis, telepathy, astral projection, pyrokinesis or telekinetics. Tessa decided they should wrap it up for the night, cover their tracks and head home. They didn't get all the answers she was hoping for, but she got some.

On the bike ride back to the farm, Tessa had plenty to contemplate. On the surface, it would seem that the mental abilities would be the easiest to hide, but they were sleeping giants. Psionic powers were deeply rooted in the subconscious and hard to control; let alone understand. They often exposed themselves in powerful, uncontrollable bursts and if she didn't know the extent of her power, then there was no possible way for her to prevent an outburst that could blow her cover. The physical abilities she would have to watch out for and make sure she didn't show any signs of enhanced strength but was another unknown physical ability which again she was at risk peeking through uncontrolled. She just had to make sure no one looked too closely, and that was going to be an enormous hurdle. With the Evo response team at the school investigating, she would have to be extra careful. They are trained to look for the slight clues or details, and they have the knowledge and the tools to spot an Evo from a mile away. Tessa was playing a dangerous game, but she had few options.

9

Tessa got very little rest that night. How could she? Tessa just learned she was a monster and a dangerous monster on top of everything. Her power rated at the highest possible level, and the worst part of all was that she wasn't sure about her full extent of power. She had the potential to cause significant harm to the people around her. She could hurt; or worse, kill her family and friends by accident. She had no clue what her power was let alone how to control it. Too much was unknown and that feeling was terrifying.

Despite her newfound abilities and the questions they posed, other issues were arising every second. Every student that was discovered to have an Evo ability was swiftly escorted from the premises and delivered into the hands of the H.I.V.E. Tessa had no idea what happened to the surrendered Evos, and there were plenty of rumors floating around to terrify her. Some stories suggest that Evos are locked away underground never again to see the light of day, too dangerous to be allowed any freedoms. Some people thought the government experimented on Evos to find weaknesses or develop weapons from their DNA. There were whispers that Evos were brainwashed and sent to fight against the rebel Evos for the H.I.V.E. And then there was the belief that the government just executed all Evos as soon as possible to remove the threat and Evo traits from contaminating the gene pool.

The unexpected that lay ahead was overwhelming, and Tessa struggled to process all the possibilities. She felt numb in her own body. Unable to focus or compose a rational thought. She felt distant, in a daze, just going through the motions. Autopilot. She was far too confused to focus on any one problem with there being so many pressing issues to address. So she felt like her brain had shut down, operating only on the simple functions. So her day began just gliding through the motions. Her fatigue from the lack of sleep made her lackadaisical and slow, but she managed to get through her morning chores and make it to school on time.

When Tessa arrived at school, she wished she had stayed in bed. The school was crawling with H.I.V.E personnel, and the bustle was significantly larger than it had been the previous day with the initial response team. They had called in reinforcements. She wondered what had changed that triggered them to send more people and she was frightened of the answer. They had nearly the whole day yesterday to collect their data and specimens and return to their labs far away from here. What compelled them to stay and bring in more people? Their remaining presence was unorthodox. Her worst fears were confirmed when she was herded into the lunch room with the rest of the students to sit quietly and await further instructions.

She was forced to sit at a table far from Sam and Arica, and the look on their faces echoed her concern. She sat next to a mousey young girl, and a quiet boy whom she had never took time to notice before. They were both levels below her in learning, but she tried to put on a happy face and tried her best to be polite. They had been here for a while already, and Tessa hoped they were observant enough to know what was going on.

She spoke carefully to them as she scanned the room for clues on what was happening. "This is odd." She said casually to spur some small talk, "I figured they would finish up yesterday and move on. What's so special here?"

The boy became excited to speak of his speculation, "I think they found something," he whispered.

"Shh…We're not supposed to be talking." The girl eyed the security that was working their rounds keeping everyone in line.

Tessa scooted closer, "What could there be to find? There was an Evo battle here, nothing else."

"They're testing early," he answered.

Tessa's fears were quickly mounting, and her palms began to sweat, "Testing for what?"

"I'm assuming they're looking for Evos."

"Why would they be looking for Evos?"

"My guess is they found some evidence that led them to believe there might have been a third Evo involved in yesterday's attack."

She sat back and took a deep breath, "Interesting." It wasn't interesting at all; it was terrifying. Today was going to be her last day here with her family and friends, and she didn't even have an opportunity to say goodbye. Torn away from everything she had ever known, and this could be her last day on earth. She had to remain calm on the outside, but she could hear her heartbeat ringing in her ears. She felt like at any moment her heart might burst and end it all right now. Falling dead on the floor. Part of her almost wished for that ending.

Tessa nervously watched as they called students back table by table to their makeshift lab beyond the lunchroom doors. When it was her turn, she was surprised she could manage to stand, let alone walk. Tessa felt so shaky that she expected to fall over at any moment, but that might raise suspicion, and so she focused on keeping her movements fluid and still. There was always that glimmer of hope that maybe everything was just a nightmare and that she would wake up safely tucked away in her bed back home.

She stood in line awaiting her turn for that needle to draw her blood and analyze her DNA. She was startled as Professor Green approached her requesting one of the H.I.V.E scientists to have a private word with her. He claimed he wanted to speak with her about Evie to make sure that she was alright after yesterday's commotion. He explained that he was afraid the young lady had been traumatized. So he pulled Tessa from the line and into his office in the corner of the lab.

He closed the door behind him, "Do you want to go with them today?"

"Excuse me, why would I go with them today."

"Tessa, I've been watching you for some time now, and I have picked up on your little secret. Your altercation the other day with Brock was all I needed to confirm my suspicions?"

She began to sweat, "I'm not sure what you mean?"

"The brick. You broke that brick with your bare hands."

"My combat training has taught me to break bricks with my hands."

"Not like this Tessa. I tested residue left at the site of contact. Do you want to know what I found?"

She swallowed, "I don't know."

"I found what they are going to find."

Tessa knew there was no escaping this but why had he pulled her away before discovered, "What are you planning to do?"

"I would like to help Tessa. You have some powerful gifts, and I work with some people who could help you discover your potential."

"Who exactly do you work for?" Tessa figured she knew the answer but wanted to hear it from his lips.

"I work for the rebels."

"And the rebels want to help me?"

"We don't have much time for this debate, but the rebels are not what the H.I.V.E would like you to believe they are. I offer you some extra time to see for yourself and decide on your own."

"What do I have to do?" She didn't have many options at the moment. This choice seemed like the only one, and maybe it could buy her enough time to figure it out her next move.

"All I ask is that you meet with the rebels and consider their offer. You don't have to take it. Just listen to the possibilities. In exchange, I will give you an injection that will mask your Evo DNA from their testing."

At this point she was desperate, and she accepted the terms of the injection. She hoped she could live to fight another day. At least this would give a few more precious moments with her family before the consequences of her choices caught up with her. Maybe the rebels could even help her determine the full extent of her powers and teach her how to control them. It was wishful thinking, but she had to hold on to some hope that her life wouldn't crumble apart in a matter of seconds.

Tessa returned to the line after the injection, under the watchful eye of the government security wondering if they were at all suspicious of the office conversation. Maybe they knew all along, and this was all an elaborate ruse. She continued to stress herself out until they had taken her blood sample and given the all clear. Her blood was devoid of any Evo DNA markers. She sighed in relief that she had passed this test and was now optimistic that she had resources to help her fool future tests as well.

At least her initial fears were momentarily suppressed with the help of Professor Green. But at what cost. She met up with her friends and explained to them the conversation leading up to her passing the Evo testing. Both Sam and Arica feared that she had made a terrible decision, but without knowing what happens to people who test positive for Evo DNA, they couldn't be sure.

Tessa's friends only focused on what they knew about the resistance of Evos. The rebel Evos were known to attack military and supply envoys and hold territories in defiance of the H.I.V.E. They were extremely dangerous and powerful, as most Evos are, but this wasn't just one Evo it was a whole organized group of them. And they collectively had one goal, to destroy the government strongholds left on the earth. There were factions all over the world, and there were several factions here in what was once America. This Midwestern faction had just recently encroached on territories closer to Oklahoma City. They currently held the Kansas City territory which meant that at some point soon she would be making the long journey to Kansas City with Professor Green's assistance.

She wasn't excited about meeting with the rebels, but there was a lack of options at the moment. They had helped her out, but she was sure they wanted something from her in return. She tested high on the Evo power scale, and she was sure their interest was in recruiting her to fight for their cause. She wasn't entirely sure what their objective was. The only information they had to go on was government propaganda which was rampant. She was never quite sure what to believe when it came from their supposed H.I.V.E leadership. Nothing ever seemed quite right. They always seemed to be trying too hard to convince people of their plans, and that made Tessa wonder how much information was spun to produce the desired result.

Tessa's friends insisted on accompanying her to the rebel base no matter how vigorously she protested. They were nervous to go, but they cared about her enough to want to protect her. Tessa had no idea how well they would be perceived if they came along, but there seemed to be no way to convince them otherwise. The rebels would have to find a way to be accommodating to humans if they wanted to attempt to recruit her. It was comforting to know that at least Tessa would have a few familiar faces in her corner to support her moving forward into this new uncharted territory.

Whether she decided to help the rebels or not, they were surely planning to rally her to their cause, and she was determined to get something in return no matter what. She had to play it careful enough to get some more of the Evo masking serum. There would be other tests, and she needed to pass them the same as this time. She was also hoping for clarification on her new abilities. Tessa was fearful of losing control or having them manifest without her being aware. The professor had promised there would be people who could help her. That was a definite reason to go. She could learn what her powers were and how to control them. More importantly, how to hide them. She was wary of the trade-off. What would be the cost of her covert education?

Tessa knew she had just entered into a dangerous game and she had to be careful not to intertwine her friends too deeply. She needed to protect them from the unforeseen consequences of her actions. She did not wish to see them suffer for her choices. She was playing a game between H.I.V.E and the rebels. She didn't want to commit to either side, but she had to appear sympathetic to both. If one found out about the other, the fallout could be epic, and her friends and family could end up caught in the crosshairs. She had to move forward cautiously and not blinded by persuasive propaganda. Tessa just needed to survive, and that quickly became her motto.

10

Life seemed to roll on by after Tessa passed the Evo DNA test and things seemed to return to normal, at least on the surface. Deep down she was still plagued with the doubt and worry about her newfound abilities. She tried to avoid using them at all but every once and a while; she had to test them out to confirm they were still there. She often used a bit of her enhanced strength when she was alone in the barn working on farm equipment. She would move large tires or pick up massive parts, and she always discovered that her Evo abilities were still there.

Tessa knew that she possessed other abilities which were mental, but she had no idea what talent she had. She was almost afraid to think, wondering if she might cause some cataclysm from a single thought. Her power was ranked at the highest rating so who knows what kind of destruction she could create with only her mind.

She did her best to appear normal on the outside when she was at school or working on the farm. As time passed, people began talking about the incident with Static Shock and Gale Force less and less. Tessa hoped that it would fade away altogether. The further behind her she could put that problem the better, but a new worry had intensified. Professor Green had not approached her about her visit to the rebels for the last few weeks following the attack; in fact, he hadn't spoken to her at all. Tessa was hoping he would forget. He was going through the school day same as her; pretending nothing happened. Maybe he did forget. Or the rebels changed their minds. No doubt, wishful thinking on her part.

One evening, she got the answer to her question as she was working alone in the barn. At least she thought she was alone when she entered her workspace. Through the eerie silence, she could hear someone or something lurking in a dark corner. They didn't stay hidden long. Once the shadowy figure confirmed that Tessa was alone, Gale Force stepped out of the shadows and into the light with her hands up in assurance of her neutrality, "I mean no harm. I'm just here to talk."

Tessa slammed some wrenches into her metal toolbox producing an echoing reverberation of metal against metal, "What makes you think I want to talk to you? You ruined my life."

Gale Force was dressed in plain clothes this time and casually took a seat at Tessa's workbench stool, "I didn't ruin your life, Tessa. You were bound to evolve with or without my encounter. It was inevitable."

"You know my name now? I didn't know we were on a first name basis. So are we friends now?"

"Depends on you. The Professor told me your name. My real name is Melanie Rain if that makes you feel any better."

Tessa fiddled with a few greasy parts juggling them nervously in her hands, "Melanie Rain huh. Seems fitting with your abilities."

"I've noticed quite a few of our real names echo our abilities."

"Tessa Jones seems pretty plain to me."

"Not everyone's name coincides with their talents, but your abilities are far from plain."

Tessa shuttered at the thought of her uniqueness, "So why are you here? Is it time to visit Kansas City?"

Melanie shook her head no, "I'm just here to talk and offer help or guidance if I can."

"I don't need any help, and I'm certainly not looking for guidance from you." Tessa turned her back to Melanie hoping she would take the hint and leave but she didn't.

"Do you think you can stay here on this farm?"

"I don't see why not?" Tessa was annoyed with the question.

"You are special, Tessa. Not only are you an Alpha Evo but Professor told us you are a strongly trained fighter and an engineering wiz."

"Well if I test out of those duties I can stay here in Ag."

"Do you think THEY haven't noticed your potential in those other areas? You can't fool them, Tessa. You fooled them into thinking you're not an Evo, but I'm sure they doubt those results. I can guarantee it."

"What do you mean?" Tessa's concern grew to paranoia as that possibility.

"The circumstances of that fight. I'm sure they figured there was another Evo involved based on the evidence they collected. They have to believe that the Evo is a student and you were present at the time. They're watching you, and you're foolish to think they're not."

Tessa looked around nervously, "Then all the more reason why you shouldn't be here right now."

"I promise I wasn't followed. I'm good at covering my tracks. Remember I fly. There aren't any tracks to cover."

"Then what else do you want?"

"Are you content to live out your days here on this farm? You have so much potential, how can you waste it all?"

"I don't see it as potential. I see it as a good way to get myself and my family killed."

"That's why you can't stay Tessa. I know you want to, but the best thing for your family is to leave."

"And join the rebel's right?"

"Maybe. It's an option, but not the only option. Plenty of Evos go off to do their own thing."

"Terrorize people?"

"Or just live."

She seemed genuine, but Tessa had her doubts, "What makes you think I'm not doing that now?"

"They will come for you. Do you know what the H.I.V.E will do with you?" Melanie stood and moved closer to Tessa.

"Do you know?" Tessa had wondered what happened to the Evos hauled away from the school.

"There are several things they might do. In your case with your fighting and engineering skills; they will most likely put you on a tact team to fight us. They will fill your head full of nonsense and warp your mind, but Tessa they don't care about Evos. They want us all gone. Even the ones who help them. They hate us. If you don't comply or you fight their conditioning, you'll end up as an experiment. They will tear you apart and use

148

your body and mind for science. They will harvest your DNA to make weapons to fight other Evos, and you are strong. They will want what the power you have. They are scared of us, and that makes them dangerous. You have to leave before they come for you."

"How do I know that's true?"

"You have to take my word for it. My brother was an Evo, and they used him up and then harvested his body for his DNA. "

"How would you know that?"

"Because I used to work for them and I escaped before they could do the same to me. I vowed to avenge my brother." There were tears in Melanie's eyes which made Tessa want to believe she was telling the truth.

Tessa was always afraid of the answer, and now that she knew, it didn't make her choices any more manageable. It made them scarier. "I'm not sure what I should do."

"Honestly it doesn't matter to me what you choose. If you chose the rebels, great help us fight to free our brothers and sisters. If you chose to run, I wish you the best. I don't want to see what happened to my brother happen to anyone else. Just think about it, please. We can't afford for your power to fall into the wrong hands."

The sun had fallen over the horizon by the time they finished their conversation and Tessa was inclined to believe Melanie to be genuine in her confessions. It didn't make the choices she faced any easier. It raised more questions than answers despite having some of her suspicions confirmed. Either option didn't seem ideal. Run or join. It appeared her hope to fade away as a farmer with her family wasn't meant to be, and she didn't want to jeopardize her family. She couldn't bare anything to happen to them because of her. They would face enough scrutiny when she left, or if they came for her. As far as she knew, she was the only one with powers in her family. They should be safe as long as they had no idea where she had gone.

She returned to the house late surprised to find the Professor sitting at the kitchen table with both her parents. They were having some tea over some idle chatter. Tessa froze like a deer in headlights in the kitchen doorway. She wasn't sure what the Professor had told her parents. Did they know about her?

Her mother waved her over to the open chair, "Tessa have a seat. We thought you would never come in from that dusty old barn you hide in all day."

She sat down, and her dad spoke up, "Professor Green has been telling us about your class science experiment."

Tessa glanced nervously at the Professor, "Don't be so modest child. I already told them about your solar power experiment and the conference in Oklahoma City."

She tried her best to play along, "Oh right, Oklahoma City." Did he know Melanie was just here? Was this all planned or was it coincidence?

"The Professor says there is a conference next week where you and some other students will be presenting their projects." Her mother seemed excited, "You know my sister went to work as a scientist with H.I.V.E." She sighed, "I haven't seen her in years."

Tessa tried to play it off, "Perhaps she will be there judging."

Her mother just shrugged it off as a faint possibility. The rest of the conversation was the Professor regaling the details of the fake trip. He even had counterfeit waivers and permission slips. He had thought of everything. Tessa sat quietly wondering how many times he had done this before. How many kids had he shipped off to the rebels? Was he a recruiter? Was he an Evo?

It seemed like he had convinced the school that this event was real and there was even a school assembly to celebrate those children "chosen" to attend. Conveniently the chosen few were Sam, Arica, and Tessa and the Professor had also worked up some elaborate prototype to pose as this solar energy device. Professor had hosted a few other assemblies like this one, and Tessa wondered if those were cover-ups for the same trip to visit the rebels. She realized that much of the life as she saw it on the surface was a lie beneath. The world was not as it appeared and it was shadowed by clout and power hungry forces. She wasn't sure she wanted to be a part of any of it, but the thought of spending the rest of her life alone in hiding was frightening. What choice did she have?

11

Tessa reluctantly packed her bag for the fake school field trip. She was filled with both dread and hope; praying that this day would never come and yet anxiously awaiting. Despite all of her wishes that her troubles would melt away, it did not come true. She had to make good on her promise to Professor Green. She had to show her face at the rebel camp and at least listen to what they had to say. Tessa wasn't sure what to pack but she borrower an armor suit and weapons from the school. It wasn't an odd request. Travel was dangerous, and school officials expected travelers to be armed and protected. She didn't want them to think it strange for her not to take weapons and armor. After all, she did have superhuman strength, but then they didn't know that, and she didn't want them to figure it out either.

The professor picked her up on a Sunday morning for their drive to Kansas City in a rickety old van. Sam and Arica were already aboard, and Tessa moved her stuff around theirs to stake out her seat for the ride. She wasn't much in the mood for conversation, but they briefly discussed the travel arrangements. They would all take up watch as they drove. Professor, of course, had the front since he was driving, Arica took the back, Sam took the right side, and Tessa took the left. They needed to watch out for any gangs that might spring up on them and try to rob them during the trip.

It was a dull ride staring out into the wasteland at all the once populated towns. Now they were just dilapidated buildings and dust, only ghosts of a former life. Tessa wondered what it would have been like to live before the ice caps melted, before the sun scorched the land, and more importantly before Evos. If she could go back in time, she had to believe that everything was different. Tessa looked out at their pitiful excuse for existence. She had to wonder what the point of it all was. Crops were failing, and food was becoming more and more scarce. Dust and debris caused more illnesses and deaths per year and bandits took whatever they could from those who couldn't defend themselves. Humanity didn't have much time left on this earth as it was; so what was the point of all the fighting and squabbling for power. There would be nothing left to rule before too long.

Tessa stared out of the van window for hours scanning the horizon. Part of her welcomed an attack. Maybe they could put her out of her misery and make her choices not matter, but she wasn't that lucky. They arrived in Kansas City with no hiccups. They drove in on the old interstate with falling signs half covered in dirt and rubble. She wondered how Professor Green knew where to go with no signs to guide the way, but he seemed to know right where to go.

They pulled into what was once the recreational part of the city before evening fell and the sun dipped below the horizon. They drove the van right up to an old mall building, and Professor Green got out of the vehicle and approached the entryway. A spotlight turned on and illuminated him where he stood with his arms held high to show compliance and that he was unarmed. Tessa and the others also exited the van slowly with arms up not to provoke any hostility. She could feel her heart beating furiously in her ears. One false move and this could be the end of their journey but the front doors opened, and a small group exited the building.

Professor Green approached, and Tessa's group trailed behind with nervous hesitation. The man in the center stood surrounded by a group of well-armed and armored individuals, and so Tessa concluded that this must be the man in charge. He was a man of larger size and stature very imposing and muscular but with an inviting smile on his face. Despite his menacing appearance, he seemed friendly and approachable.

He was excited to see them, and he shook Professor Green's hand and pulled him in for a very manly hug, "I trust your trip went well."

"We had no problems."

"And which one is our Evo?" He looked beyond Green to the three of them still hesitantly approaching.

"Tessa." Professor Green called her forward.

She stepped up to the towering man, and she reached out a hand to his, "Harland Stonewell, glad to meet you."

She shook his hand, "Tessa Jones."

"Tessa we are honored to have you here to visit. This is an area of free thinking and no judgment. You are free to be who you are here." She could see Gale Force just inside the door waving hello. At least Tessa knew someone here, but she still wasn't sure if her new acquaintance could be trusted. Tessa didn't see much choice, of course, so she followed Mr. Stonewell into their facility for the tour.

Harland was proud of their newest establishment and noted several security features although he made note that they had several classified features to be doubly sure of their safety. Tessa could tell he wanted her to feel safe and at ease here but nothing about this place made her comfortable. The stone cold interior was not inviting. It was overbearing and intimidating, but they had tried to lighten the mood with colorful art and a diverse atmosphere. The people here indeed seemed free with brightly colored hair and progressive clothing. Most of the people were young not much older than herself. Mr. Stonewell and Professor Green were among the oldest in the building by far.

Their tour guide explained the organization as a place of learning and development. Evos could explore their talents among their peers without persecution. They could train and hone their skills before leaving on assignment elsewhere in the world. Tessa learned that Professor Green was, in fact, an Evo assigned to her school as a recruiter. She wasn't sure how she felt about that charade. Part of her believed him to be a liar waiting like a predator in the school to scoop up Evos, but another part of her wanted to believe that he was saving them from a worse fate. She wasn't sure what was real and what was a lie anymore. Her world was too upside down at the moment to make heads or tails out of anything.

The facilities were impressive with all the latest tech and areas for sparring and weapons training. Much of the tech looked like homebrewed configurations like Tessa's googles, but there was some stolen tech that looked like government-issued weapons and armor. Arica seemed enthused over the lab areas and Sam with the training facilities. Even though they were not Evos, they were both welcomed with the same regards as she was. It didn't seem to be because of her everyone seemed genuinely inviting. Mr. Stonewell informed them that several humans had volunteered to serve the rebellion. Tessa never imagined humans would sign up for the resistance if they didn't have Evo powers. Most humans hated Evos. She didn't know anyone who trusted Evos. Professor explained that there were Evos who used their skills to save lives and Evos saved many of the people working here. The notion was one she had not personally experienced, but Gale Force was trying to eliminate Static Shock who was a threat to humans. He was an Evo abusing his power.

Tessa was still uncertain, and she would have to see that the rebel's actions backed up all that they were claiming. People could say anything they wanted, but what mattered to her was their actions. She was skeptical of everything and needed to remain so, lest she gets sucked into their propaganda. Talk was cheap. She was looking for action and answers.

They wasted no time in getting down to the latter. After the tour, she arrived in the lab for testing. They wanted to get a clear picture of her abilities. Arica was immediately taken in by the lab tech, and she latched on to the scientist running the tests. At least Arica could keep a watch over her procedures and ensure that she was getting all of the information available. Perhaps Arica could even learn more about Evos than the school could teach; after all, there was an abundance of subjects here.

Tessa started with the same tests Arica conducted, a blood test and a brainwave scan and they took that data to determine what if any further analysis was needed. Arica was amazed that they had more specific Evo genetic markers mapped out than she could have ever imagined. Arica disappeared into the lab following the lab techs asking a million questions. Tessa looked at Sam who promised not to leave her side. Of course, so did the Professor and Mr. Stonewell but Tessa wasn't sure she trusted either of them and having Sam around was comforting.

Nothing about the process was comfortable and being hooked up to probes and machines was not her idea of a relaxing evening. They had promised that she was free here, but she felt more and more confined by the moment. They had moved on from the preliminary tests and on to stress tests on a treadmill hooked to wires, an MRI, and a CAT scan. After they finished violating her privacy, they allowed her and Sam to sit down at a conference table in the lab to await the final results. Her nerves were on edge, and her palms began to sweat. She licked her lips, thirsty and dry. The anticipation was absolute agony as she awaited their results.

Arica returned with a team of scientist and piles of papers. A holographic projection was transmitted from a device in the center console of the table with her test results. Tessa understood the results. She had learned to interpret at school, especially the ones her and Arica had reviewed together, but there was quite a bit on the screen she had no clue what she was seeing. Professor Green began to discuss the findings, "As Arica has already informed you, you have both physical and mental ability manifestations. Your primary physical ability is your enhanced strength of which you are already aware. The secondary ability is what we call a 'blink' ability. It's similar to enhanced speed but with a smaller duration and range. You can move from one location to another in the blink of an eye, but it is for a short duration and not as far or as prolonged as a true speedster." Tessa wiggled in her chair nervously, "As for the mental ability, it is far more complex and is the reason for your Alpha categorization. Now the physical abilities are nothing to take lightly. Having two physical abilities is an impressive feat, but adding a metal ability like this in the mix puts you in a category all your own. In honesty, you don't have a category."

She burst, "Stop beating around the bush and tell me. How bad is it?"

Mr. Stonewell interjected, "It's not BAD, Tessa. It's amazing. You're the next step in Evo evolution."

She ignored him rolling her eyes and returning her gaze to Professor Green, "Your cells are in a constant state of flux feeding on all the energy surrounding you. You can harness that raw power into a variety of manifestations. I'm not sure the full extent of your ability to manipulate this power. It appears as though you can use telekinesis to move objects with your mind, but it also looks like you can harness the raw power as a weapon."

Arica chimed in to elaborate, "The purple energy from your hands when you fought Static Shock."

Tessa looked down at her hands like they were going to jump up and bite her, "Can I control it? What if I don't want to be a weapon?"

Mr. Stonewell stepped up to the projections and zeroed in on the fluxing cells, "I'm not going to lie to you Tessa because you are far too important for that. I know you don't trust me, so I'm not going to make it worse. Learning to use this mental ability is not going to come easily. We don't have anyone in our ranks with a power even close to yours. We do have psychics like the Professor here and a technopath but not someone who has access to raw power as you do. I want to warn you that powers of this nature can be dangerous."

Tessa swallowed that bit of news hard, and carefully asked her next question, "You have the gene suppression meds, is there a permanent cure."

Since the professor knew her better, Mr. Stonewell allowed him to address her request, "Here, being an Evo and having these gifts are a blessing. We have the means to make a difference in the world."

"It sounds like this ability is not a gift. Answer the question." She grew aggravated by his redirection.

"We don't have a cure, Tessa. We don't want a cure."

"We? Is there a cure somewhere else?"

Silence filled the room. No one wanted to answer the question, but Mr. Stonewell finally did, "There are rumors that the H.I.V.E has a cure but the source is unconfirmed."

Tessa stood up from the chair and nearly fell over. The crushing weight of her condition was almost too much for her to bare. She could feel the world around her quake with uncertainty. At first, Tessa thought she disoriented, but as she scanned the room, she could see the lab techs holding on to equipment to keep it from shaking off the table onto the floor. Tessa grabbed her head as pain shot through her brain, and she struggled to see clearly. A lab tech spoke out to Mr. Stonewell, "Her power is unstable; she shouldn't be here."

Sam and Professor Green steadied her, and the shaking stopped, and they lead her to a set of living quarters. There wasn't much but some tables, chairs, and cots but at least she could lie down for a moment and have a quiet moment to think. The room was spinning out of control almost as quickly as her life. She was a danger to herself and everyone around her. She needed a cure. She needed it now.

12

Tessa locked herself away for nearly the entire day within the confines of their temporary living quarters. If she stepped outside, it reminded her of why she was here. Tessa would once again have to deal with the reality that she was an Evo. The thought of a cure was mildly comforting; however, she didn't want to take her chances with the H.I.V.E to find out. There were far too many things that could go wrong.

Sam and Arica had no problems leaving the room to mingle with the Evos. They seemed to have overcome their initial fears, but then they weren't the ones coping with newfound abilities that they didn't wish to have. If the shoe was on the other foot, they might react differently. Sam finally coaxed her from her out of hiding. He described the training facilities to her and persuaded her into some combat therapy. At first, she was reluctant. What if she lost control of her abilities? After consideration, she decided that people here were capable of dealing with her powers and it was probably something they dealt with from time to time. Although not at level alpha strength. Maybe it would scare them into leaving her alone or lead them to agree that she was too dangerous and needed the cure.

She apprehensively left the confines of their room to visit the training facilities of which Sam spoke so highly. She had put on her armor, boots and custom goggles hung around her neck just in case she needed them. There were several sectioned off areas for different types of training. There were sections for firearms and archery as well as hand to hand mixed martial arts fighting rings. There were already Evos training in all of the areas, and she watched as the vibrant young Evos honed their skills. She saw a wide range of Evo abilities as she strolled through the facility. She noticed camouflaging, flames, ice, and several others that she couldn't identify or name. There were many different talents in the room, but they all noticed her. It was as if she had a thousand eyes watching her as she walked through the training grounds.

She stopped at an unoccupied sparring ring. Tessa wasn't sure she was ready for sparring just yet, but there were punching bags and dummies. She started her work out there, and it was a much-needed stress reliever. Tessa took to striking and kicking the punching bag and worked on her attack combos. She became more and more focused on the bag as she progressed and her attacks became more and more aggressive. She was working through all that pent-up anger and frustration until she landed a blow so hard that the punching bag broke away from its mount and hurled across the training floor crashing into a wall with a thunderous boom that echoed through the building.

She stopped and breathed deeply regaining her composure. As she did, she looked around to discover that a crowd had formed around her training ring. She had acquired an audience that she wished to hide from now. They now knew that she had no control over her power, but they weren't running. Instead, they were watching and waiting to see what she was going to do next.

Mr. Stonewell stepped forward clapping his hands in approval, "Very good. You are a trained fighter, and your strength serves you well. Let's see if we can't coax out some of those other abilities. "Derik," he called out to the group. "Can someone find Derik and get him over here."

Tessa shyly approached him and tried begging quietly for forgiveness. "I'm sorry. I didn't mean to break it."

"No worries. I do it all the time."

"Right. I'm not sure fighting is the best activity for me at the moment. I seem unable to control myself."

"Perfect. That's exactly what we want." He waved over a wiry young man with shaggy brown hair and a crooked smile.

"Derik, suit up. See that Miss Tessa's blink ability shows itself. She's a trained fighter with an accompanying strength ability." He patted the boy on the back, and he disappeared to get prepped. Stonewell turned back around to speak with Tessa, "Derik is a speedster Tessa, and he's going to test your boundaries a little to see if we can find that blink ability from your genetics test. No worries about hurting him. Doubt you can catch him in the first place and even if you did he heals lightning fast with the help of equally fast metabolism."

Derik returned in a black training suit ready to spar, but Tessa was still unsure of herself. Mr. Stonewell was pushing her, and she didn't like it. "What am I supposed to do?"

Mr. Stonewell exited the training area and shouted back to her, "Try to stay on your feet."

Tessa stepped into the ring with a sigh as she accepted this challenge for which she didn't feel ready. This situation was precisely what she didn't want to happen. She should have stayed in the room. Lesson learned. As soon as she could retreat to the solitude of the room, the better off she would be; so she stepped up to get it over with.

Derik joined her on the mat but remained at the far end as she awaited him to join her in the center. She shrugged at him wondering if he wasn't interested in sparring, but as she did, he seemed to disappear in a streak of white lightning before her eyes. In a swift second and a gust of air, she found herself on the ground with the wind knocked from her lungs. She looked around the mat to Derik on the opposite edge of the mat waving at her with that crooked, mischievous smile. Tessa pulled herself back to her feet and readied her stance. Again swept off her feet before she even knew what hit her. This took place quite a few times, and some of the spectators got bored watching. As she continued to pick herself up off the floor, she wondered if the genetics test was wrong. Maybe she didn't have this power they thought she did and that gave her hope that perhaps they were wrong about other things as well.

She started to get sore from all the falling, and her aggravation grew as she tried to anticipate his moves and attempted to attack. She decided to employ the use of the goggles to see if that would give her any advantage. All she got in response was taunts from Derik, "You think glasses are going to help you see me?"

She called back, "You afraid I might make you look bad?"

He flashed her another smile, and that was the last straw. Tessa focused the goggles; calculating the projected paths of attack with an algorithmic calculation to determine probability. With her focus on knocking him down, she awaited his next strike. When he did, Tessa made her move, and she could feel something new awaken inside her. She sidestepped out his path with alarming reflexes and speed. She noticed Mr. Stonewell on edge as she could feel herself on the verge of harnessing this new power.

As much as she didn't want to be an Evo and use her abilities, she couldn't help but feel the power coursing through her veins. It was a raw strength that made her want to reach out for more. The human desire to want to feel invincible and strong. Derik moved to attack again, and this time she let go of her inhibition. She embraced that power she felt within herself again, and this time Tessa moved toward him. In the blink of an eye, she traversed from one end of the mat to the opposite end as he moved simultaneously toward her. When Derik reached where Tessa had once been on the mat, he turned around surprised to see her all the way on the other side.

Tessa focused again as she saw the competitive anger in his eyes. She had seen it before when sparring; that moment when a girl is about to best a boy in a combat sport. Tessa took a deep breath and blinked forward toward him as he sped straight at her. This time she made contact on purpose with her hand to his throat. He stopped abruptly in front of her with surprise in his eyes. Adrenaline coursed through her and she lifted him up and slammed his body to the floor.

Derik moved slowly in pain, but it wasn't long before he turned onto his back to look up and her, "Nice. I wasn't sure you had it in you."

Tessa extended a hand to help him up, "I was hoping I didn't."

"Don't fear your power. Embrace it as a gift." He pulled himself up and patted her on the back.

Mr. Stonewell approached her with satisfaction on his face, "How did it feel?"

"Unnatural." Tessa wasn't sure she would ever get used to that feeling.

"You'll get used to it." He patted her on the shoulder in assurance although it didn't change her mind or increase her confidence. She still had the same doubts as before, but now she had another ability to worry about controlling.

There was still the matter of the mental ability that scared Tessa to her core, and Stonewell had every intention of ousting that power while he had her out in the open before she could retreat back to solitude. Tessa figured he knew that if he let her return to their quarters that she would be unlikely to show her face again.

Stonewell summoned Professor Green to assist with the metal part of her power since she was a psionic Evo. His ability was different from hers, but they lacked someone who could help her with her specific type of power. The professor was one of the only people with a mental ability who might be able to help her. He took her to a cold and sterile lab room, and they sat at a table across from each other staring at each other for an uncomfortable moment. He didn't know how to teach her and no idea where to begin. So he started with meditation which Tessa found aggravating. She was always trying to get out of her head; why on earth would she want to dive deeper. She humored his efforts trying to look deep into herself for a power she wished wasn't there. He tried various concentration and focus techniques outside the realm of meditation with no luck. Tessa could tell after a few hours that he had become frustrated with her lack of progress. He even went so far as to scold her for being an unwilling pupil, which was partially correct. Tessa didn't want this psionic ability to surface.

Green wrapped up the lesson with no success and met with Mr. Stonewell outside the room. They conversed for some time before Stonewell opened the door and asked Tessa to follow. She reluctantly complied and followed him through the meandering halls deeper and deeper into their base. As they walked further into the base, there were fewer and fewer people, and the hallways were quiet and dark. She could hear her footsteps echo through the building as she wondered where they headed. Stonewell stopped just in front of a set of large metal doors with a keypad entry lock. He turned to her and took a deep breath, "I was hoping Green could teach you, but I'm not surprised he couldn't. Your power is worlds different from his. I guess I was hoping for him to make some connection. We do have one person who has an ability somewhat close to yours but I warn you he's not the most polished stone here by far. His name is Finn, and he is what we call a technopath. In layman's terms, he can control technology with his mind, which is as close as we can get to your psionic abilities. I have little confidence in his interpersonal skills to teach you, but we can't very well try nothing to help you with your powers."

With that introduction, he turned to enter the passcode on the keypad. Tessa turned her head away to avoid memorizing the combination. The less she knew about this place, the better. She was already the most powerful Evo here, and she didn't need to give them any more reasons to fear her. The steel doors unlocked with a hissing sound of pressure escaping from the other side. Stonewell entered first, and she followed him. This person sounded a little unhinged, and she wasn't sure what she was about to witness. The room was booming with machinery and computers. Many of them were moving about on their own, and some seemed to be repairing themselves or each other. There were military vehicles and aircraft in the vast hanger area that were pulling themselves apart and then back together.

Mr. Stonewell called out, "Finn!"

Tessa heard a bang and a scramble from atop some scaffolding but could only make out the outline of a shadow in the shape of a person. A man's voice boomed, "What the hell do you want? I'm working as fast as I can." He floated out from the scaffolding suspended in mid-air and descended to the floor in front of them. Tessa must have had wide eyes, and her bottom jaw must have dropped to the floor, "Who's the newbie?" He picked up a shop towel and started wiping oil from his hands.

"You would think that since you don't have to touch the machines, you wouldn't get so dirty."

"I like working with my hands, and I don't mind getting dirty." He winked at Tessa, and she snapped back to reality as her cheeks turned red with embarrassment. He was a younger man maybe in his early twenties with wavy blond hair and bright blue eyes. Tessa blushed only a little from his flirtatious comment and then she returned to her stern exterior. "So serious," he teased.

"This is Tessa. She has come to us for help. She has recently discovered that she has Evo talents."

"Lucky her," Tessa could sense sarcasm in his voice, and she started to like him. If he disliked being an Evo as much as she did, perhaps she had found an ally. "What could I possibly help with?" He reached behind a Humvee to pick up a couple of tools.

"She's psionic possibly telekinetic," Stonewell explained.

Finn peeked up over the body of the vehicle eyeing her sideways with a grin, "Really, a mental talent?" He turned over a wrench in his hands.

"Green tried working with her and got nowhere."

Finn pointed the wrench at Stonewell, "That's because Green's an idiot."

"Finn! He's a valuable asset."

"That might be true but he's a psychic, and she's a psionic. Two different beasts and he's smart enough to know that."

"He does but..."

"But I'm your last resort huh. I'm the last person you wanted to ask for help." He jumped up to sit on a nearby workbench, and a flying drone delivered him an apple that he immediately began to consume. "What about you?" He addressed Tessa with his face full of food.

She panicked for a moment in surprise, "What about me?"

"You're here to harness this talent you can't seem to manage. What's the problem?"

Stonewell stepped in to explain, "She's an Alpha."

He choked on the apple a bit and jumped down moving in close examining her up and down, "Shut up! An Alpha?"

"She has enhanced strength and can blink."

"And psionic? That's a lot of power in one body. That's scary." He backed away.

Tessa was tired of their bantering, "That's exactly what I am. Scared. I didn't ask for this."

Finn chuckled, "Nobody ever does."

"Are you going to help me or not?" Tessa was growing tired of his games.

"Are you going to kill me in the process?"

"I can't make any promises." She crossed her arms in front of her. "Keep asking like an ass, and maybe I'll have an accident."

"I like her." He pointed at her with a smile.

"Well?" Tessa wanted to see what he had to say or if he could help her.

"Alright. You've convinced me."

Stonewell spent the next few minutes giving him a full diagnostic of her condition and instructions on being a decent teacher. The words seemed to go in one ear and right out the other as Finn ignored nearly everything he said. Tessa could tell by the tension that the two didn't get along well, but it seemed like they both needed one another, so they managed to tolerate each other on some bizarre dysfunctional level. As they conversed, Tessa walked around the shop examining

Finn's work. At least this place reminded her of home, and her of her quaint little barn back on the farm. They had only been here a day, and she already longed to return home. What was going to happen when she had to leave home for good?

After Stonewell left, the real fun began. Stonewell was right; Finn was a terrible teacher, but she could tell he knew a lot about his ability. After all, there wasn't anyone here to teach him when he discovered this technopathic ability. Finn had to learn his power all on his own which couldn't have been easy. On the flip side, he didn't have two other physical abilities to balance in addition to his mental abilities, but he could fly, and that was pretty cool.

13

Tessa sat around and observed as Finn finished up what he was working on in the shop. He talked to her a little as he went about his work. Tessa discovered that Finn was the base mechanic since his ability intertwined with technology. He worked on more than just vehicles and aircraft. Finn also worked on computers, comms, weapons, and armor. Anything that had any aspect of technology to it he could repair. Tessa made small talk and told him that she worked on farm equipment back home. She figured he would find it trivial, but he seemed excited that she knew her way around an engine. He put her to work finishing a tune up on one of the Humvees. It made her feel at ease working on something with her hands. Something familiar. Her life had been changing so rapidly that it felt nice to slow down and get back the basics of what she enjoyed most.

When he finished what he was working on or at least to a good stopping point, he sat down at the workbench with her and they started in on her powers. "So what do you know about these powers? Have you ever used them before?"

"Once, but I didn't realize I was."

"Not uncommon. What were you doing when they activated?"

"Fighting an Evo."

He perked up, "You didn't know you were an Evo at the time?"

"Not at that time."

"So let me get this straight. You were fighting an Evo as a human not knowing you had powers." She shook her head, "You got balls girl. Alright so explain to me what happened when you used the powers for the first time?"

"After the fight was over..."

"When you mean over, you mean when you killed the other Evo right?"

"Yes, I killed him... but I used my gun." Those words felt strange leaving her mouth, but it didn't phase

Finn much, "Right before I shot him I looked down, and my hands had this purple glow to them, and there was an invisible force that seemed to hold him pinned to the wall."

"Nice," he exclaimed.

"What's so nice about killing someone?"

"Not that, your purple glow isn't just a basic telekinetic power. It's more akin to harnessing potential energy and converting it into kinetic energy. You can apply kinetic energy wherever potential energy exists and apply it to an object, which is way better than telekinesis."

"If you say so." It all sounded terrible to Tessa.

"Do you understand the basic physics of potential and kinetic energy?"

"Yes. I work on engines. It's engineering mechanics 101."

He could feel her uneasiness, "Look I get it. I had a hard time at first too. Still, do sometimes. But it doesn't go away, and the quicker you can learn to live with it the better."

"What if I hurt someone?"

185

He shrugged, "The best thing you can do is to embrace the power and accept it. Learn how to use it so you can always be in control. That way you don't hurt anyone. This type of power…," he pointed to his head, "is scariest I think. The mind is a powerful thing, and I don't think we know all there is to know when it comes to cognitive function. The one thing I can say is that you came to the right place to learn."

"Do you like it here?" Tessa pulled him a little off subject, but she was curious to know.

He hesitated, "Look I'll give you the straight answer cause that's the one you deserve. Don't get caught up in all the hype because they're gonna want ya here. You're an Alpha. Do what you want and what feels right. I can say I'd rather be here than on the other side. I've seen what they do on the other side, and it's not pretty."

She swallowed hard at the thought of the government options she had been warned about, "Someone told me that they know about me and that my family won't be safe with me around."

"If the H.I.V.E knows about you, then it's only a matter of time before they come for you. You'll have to choose this rebel life or a runaway." He shrugged but didn't have a suggestion about which option she should choose. She appreciated him not trying to pressure her and telling her the truth. This choice had its flaws just like any other, but it was the choice he had made so there must be something he likes about this place.

Once Tessa was more at ease, Finn started working with her to coax out her powers. She found that being comfortable and trusting him more than some of the others helped her move past her apprehensions and embrace these skills much more naturally. It made logical sense that she would have to learn the powers to be able to control them and so she felt willing to try.

Finn explained her power very differently from the professor, rather than focusing internally he had her focus on outward energy. He explained that potential energy was all around her just waiting for her to seize. Energy was present in the air or objects which stored it for later use. She had direct access to the stored energy and could put it to use however she could imagine. The possibilities were endless. She was only limited by her imagination. What made it all click for her was that he explained it in terms that she could understand. He described her power in terms of a combustion engine; she was the fuel igniting everything around her. That made sense to her. She was the catalyst for the reaction causing potential energy to become kinetic energy. She reached out to feel the power waiting in the space surrounding her. Her hands began to glow faintly purple, and she got nervous which caused her to lose focus and drop control.

Finn congratulated Tessa on harnessing the power and encouraged her to try again but with more focus. He told her to let the fear go and let the power flow through her freely. The more she fights, the harder the process becomes and increases the probability of something going wrong. Tessa recollected her composure and began her focus again. This time the purple grow was brighter and stronger.

"Perfect! Now hold that and focus on the wall over there. Throw your energy from your hands to the wall. Sometimes physical movement helps with the control, especially at first."

She did just as he asked and a burst of bright purple energy exploded from her hand hurling toward the wall where it exploding upon contact. There was a charred mark left on the wall where the blast had hit.

"That's how you can use your power as a blast weapon. It is pure energy, and you control how it reacts. Now you can also use the power within an object as well. This time take the apple and channel your energy into it like you're charging a battery," Finn handed her an apple. She did as he instructed and charged the apple with the glowing purple energy. "Now this apple is full of the energy you control, so you control the apple. Move the apple from your hands to float in the space just over there near the wall." She moved the apple with her mind as he requested, "Now ignite that energy and explode the apple." She did as he asked. "You are a natural at this my dear. You feel that power with little effort. Your greatest enemy is in your mind, Tessa. If you could let go of those fears inside you, there would be nothing you couldn't do with this power."

"That is what I'm afraid of."

"Understandable. Power is a massive weight of responsibility, but you can't change the fact that you have this power. So you have to respect the responsibility and try your best to make the right choices. There's no clear-cut handbook in this world about how to be a good Evo. Just do the best you can. That's the best advice I can give."

"Thank you for treating me like a normal person."

He chuckled, "Well we are still just people. Normal is a relative term. Some people let their power go to the head. Stay grounded Tessa."

She spent the rest of the day in the shop working on the equipment alongside Finn and using her power off and on as she got more comfortable with the idea. Finn had a fantastic collection of LP's, and Tessa trolled through his collection listening to everything new she could get her hands on as they worked. She fell instantly in love with Led Zeppelin and their bluesy folkish tones. For the first time in a long while, Tessa felt relaxed and free in this safe space. It was refreshing not to hide from anyone, and she could be herself. She was just Tessa with all of her strengths and weakness, and Finn left her to her own business and gave her the space she needed. No one was breathing down her neck wondering if her power was going to destroy them or what she might be capable of doing. There were no expectations here, and that was a marvelous feeling. She could see why Finn liked to keep this space to himself. He didn't seem to mind her there, but she didn't want to overstay her welcome, so she would finish up working on the Humvee and return to her room.

As she was finishing up rotating the tires on the Humvee using the assistance of her power, she was startled by Mr. Stonewell who had snuck up behind her. She wasn't sure how she missed him. Perhaps she was too focused on her power or the music or maybe a combination. She dropped the tire from the Humvee positioned on the lift and jumped with an audible squeak.

"I see Finn was able to teach you to use your power."

She shrugged and blushed a little. She wasn't ready for other people to see her use her power but it seemed a little too late in this case. "Yeah, it was pretty easy once he explained it in a way I could understand."

He left Tessa to find Finn, and she watched from a distance as they had a seemingly heated conversation. Whatever Mr. Stonewell was proposing; Finn wasn't in agreeance, and she was about to find out as they both came back toward her. Mr. Stonewell began, "Tessa we are planning an op tonight to raid a compound northeast of Oklahoma City, near the Stillwater area."

"That's a dead zone." She knew that area to be quarantined by the government for some toxic radiation from the Black Fox nuclear reactor meltdown.

"They want us to believe that it's a contaminated area to keep us out, but we've sent a team to test the area, and there is no trace of radiation. What is there; a H.I.V.E base that we believe is a laboratory, and we intend to find out what they're working on there. We have reason to believe they are conducting tests on Evos."

She looked at Finn, who didn't seem keen on her going, "How do you know they're working on anything at all?" She inquired.

"We don't know for sure, but that's why we need to send a team in to investigate. I thought you might like to know what happens to the Evos the H.I.V.E collects."

She pondered the option. On the one hand, this op sounded like a dangerous long shot, but then again she was curious about what happened to the Evos that the H.I.V.E hauled off. She deferred to Finn, "What do you think?"

He perked up and seemed pleased that she consulted him, "I think it's a bad idea. You just learned to use your power today, and he wants to send you into combat. The stress could cause your power to become unstable."

Mr. Stonewell interjected, "She's proficient in combat even without her powers."

"And she's also an Alpha who doesn't have full control yet. You don't know what might happen if she's pushed too far. Not only is that dangerous to her but it could go poorly for the whole team. It's reckless and puts a lot of lives at risk."

Tessa thought about her options and asked Finn, "Are you going on the op?"

"Yes," he answered bluntly.

"Do you think I should go or not?"

"Remember what I told you earlier? You decide what's best for you."

"If I go, can you stay close to me and help me if I need it?"

He nodded in affirmation, but she still wasn't sure what she should do, "I'll have to think about it Mr. Stonewell, but thank you for the invite."

He seemed content with the answer but not overly pleased. At least it wasn't a flat out no. Finn had blocked him from getting what he wanted, and he seemed like the kind of man who always got what he wanted. That's why he was the leader of this faction. That didn't mean that he had anyone other than his own best interests at heart. Tessa had to weigh how comfortable she felt with entering a potential combat scenario as a brand new Alpha Evo. She still lacked the confidence in her ability to control her powers, but the pull of curiosity was outweighing her common sense logic.

By the end of the day and after a lengthy discussion with Finn, she concluded that she would join them on the op. She took the remaining time before departure to meet up with her friends and bring them up to speed on her evening plans. It seemed like they were enjoying their stay despite being a minority surrounded by powered individuals. Sam enjoyed in the weapons tech and equipment they had developed here, and Arica loved the scientific aspects of the operation. They were both very talented at their prospective studies, and Tessa was glad to see they were mingling and fitting in with Evos. After all, she was an Evo, and so they were forced to think about Evos in a different light given their best friend was now one.

She left them to their own devices and went about her own. She headed to the cafeteria for a quick bite and a chance to try interacting with other Evos. Unfortunately, she found the latter difficult. Sam and Arica seemed to blend right in, but Tessa felt like she stuck out like a sore thumb. She could feel eyes on her the moment she entered the cafeteria. The feeling was unnerving. As she walked by tables with her tray full of food, groups stopped talking as she passed. Once she was gone, they would start talking again but then in a whisper. It seemed that everyone here knew who she was but she didn't know anyone.

She searched for a quiet spot to sit when she noticed an arm that seemed to be waving her over. Thank god it was Melanie aka Gale Force, at least someone was friendly toward her. She sat across from Melanie looking awkwardly behind her at the crowds of people who were gossiping about her behind her back.

"Don't mind them. They've never seen an Alpha before, and they heard about your match with Derik earlier. Plus they know you visited Finn and no one ever sees him. He's not the friendly sort if you haven't noticed." She continued to eat as she talked.

"Are you going on the op tonight?"

She stopped eating in surprise, "How do you know about the op?"

"Mr. Stonewell asked me if I wanted to go. So you are going right?"

"Yeah. I'll be there."

"Can you help Finn keep an eye on me? I'm worried about losing control of my powers, but I'm curious about what we might find."

She leaned in, "How's the power coming along?"

She forgot to tell her about her success, "I can control it...somewhat."

"Perfect. Then you should be fine tonight. Just stay focused. I can help."

Tessa sighed in relief at knowing she now had two people to watch her back, "What's the deal with Finn anyway?"

"I don't know the whole story. All I do know is that Finn and Stoney don't see eye to eye. I'm not sure on what exactly, but it seems like they fight on every decision. They butt heads constantly. I think Finn wants space to himself and Stonewell has other plans for him. Finn is always worried that his powers are being used and abused and so if he doesn't find the task suitable or he feels exploited then he refuses."

"Do you think Mr. Stonewell oversteps the line ever?"

Her eyes darted back and forth taking note of the people around her, and she lowered her voice, "Sometimes I feel like his agenda is a little off balance and his methods are questionable at times, but I don't feel like he's ever outright used other Evos or me for that matter. He tows a thin line sometimes, but we are at war, and someone has to make the difficult decisions. Sometimes he makes the right decisions sometimes not, but we're still here so it can't be all bad. If you're asking what I think of all this, I choose this because the alternative is far worse. We have to stop the H.I.V.E from enslaving, and murdering Evos and I would choose this side over and over again if given another choice."

"Maybe I'll have more answers tonight after the op." She was hoping to discover the motives of the H.I.V.E, and that could help her decide what to do with her life. She accepted the fact that she could no longer stay at home, but she wasn't sure this option was any better. Stonewell seemed eager to have her on board but was that because she was one of them or because she is an Alpha. There were far too many unanswered mysteries at this time for her to make a decision yet.

"Any thought of a name."

She hesitated in confusion, "Name?"

"Yeah. Like Gale Force." She put her fists on her hips and pushed out her chest, posing like a champion.

"I'm not sure I need a name." She chuckled.

"Sure you do. Everyone has one."

"What's Finn's," she inquired.

She frowned, "He doesn't count."

"Why not?"

"He's different. Just think about it," Melanie got up to leave.

"What like Strong Blinking Mental Girl?" She was obviously facetious.

"That's a little much. I think you should go back to the drawing board on that one. Maybe 'Joule' as in a measurement of energy." She shrugged, "I may or may not have been thinking about that one for a while. Mull it around and let me know what you think. I think it could stick."

She left Tessa to clean up what was left of her meal and finish her preparations for the op. She left the cafeteria and the whispering gossips behind her and set out on a new adventure. She was scared of what might happen, and the nerves made her stomach churn with excitement. That was just it. She wasn't just scared. She was excited too. This place was a new chapter in her life. Whatever happened tonight could be a defining moment for her and could shape her future choices. She had to choose a path, and lately, everything was leading up to this moment. The air felt electrified with anticipation of what the future might hold. For the first time in a long time, Tessa was hopefully optimistic.

14

Tessa reported to Finn's hanger bay at the designated time to embark on the mission. There she found both Finn and Melanie suiting up for the job; along with the Derick the speedster from earlier. Tessa had dressed in her suit back in her room, so she was all ready to go armor, weapons and all. The only thing she required was comms. Tessa noticed the other members of the team as well including Professor Green. There was another woman who introduced herself as Vanessa Green and confirmed she was the professor's wife.

Stonewell was at the center of it all and smiled when he noticed that Tessa had joined the group, "Glad to see you join us, Tessa."

She glanced at Finn nervously, "I'm here to observe and not to fight."

Stonewell nodded in agreeance, "Whatever you prefer my dear."

Tessa wanted to make sure she was clear in drawing that line in the sand. She was curious about what secrets they might find in the H.I.V.E labs, but she was not inclined to conclude that joining the rebels was the best choice. She continued to remind herself the value of remaining neutral.

Finn patted her on the back supportively, and they all boarded the hovercraft. It was a rectangular shape with several horizontal fan-like propellers jutting from the sides to create the needed lift. The exterior was dark black and glowed blue indicating electrical power which illuminating faintly under the hanger fluorescents. Tessa could sense the energy coursing through the aircraft with her new found ability. The engine blades were stealthy and quieter than any helicopter she had ever encountered, including the helos she had seen arriving at the school after her run-in with Static Shock. This engineering design was cutting edge and rivaled that of even H.I.V.E military technology. Undoubtedly a benefit of having a technopath as the base mechanic.

The back hatch was down and ready for the team to board. The hull of the aircraft had seats along the interior to the left and right with harnesses for each seat. There were six seats with three along each side. Professor Green and Mr. Stonewell assumed the pilot and co-pilot seats in the front control area and the rest of the crew filled the hull seats. Tessa chose the side with her friends Finn and Melanie, and they helped her with the harness. Equipped with carbineers and ropes, the harness attached to the hull behind and above her head. Melanie explained that the center of the aircraft floor opened and that the team would deploy by cable from the opening. The aircraft did not need to land and could circle the perimeter to ensure safety during the mission. It could return for their extraction when needed. Melanie seemed confident which meant the team had done this many times before.

Finn introduced her to the comms which consisted of a wireless mic to pick up vocals for transmission and an earpiece to hear the rest of the team. Again the whole process seemed routine, and it made Tessa fell a little more comfortable with the mission. She was suited up with her armor, goggles, pistol, batons and now wired into her team. She also had all of her Evo abilities as a backup in case the op went sideways. She took a deep breath and tried to relax as the crew finished belting in and the back hatch was sealed.

No matter how hard Tessa tried to relax, she was still a nervous wreck for the entire flight. The flight itself was smooth and quick, but she felt those butterflies in her stomach and time seemed to stand still as she waited. She had nothing help her pass the time except her own thoughts which she considered dangerous. The rest of the group seemed to be relaxing before they deployed a sign of seasoned soldiers. There was no music to listen to except the faint humming of the hover engines. Tessa fired up her goggles and a music playlist to entertain her for the duration of the flight. Finn had his eyes closed and leaned back in his chair like he was sleeping. Surely he wasn't able to sleep through all this anticipation, but then again seemed different than everyone else, and he very well could sleep through it all.

After about an hour that seemed like an eternity in the air, Mr. Stonewell came over the aircraft PA to announce that they were ten minutes from the target drop zone. The announcement prompted everyone to wake up and make any last minute preparations. Tessa made one final check of all her gear to ensure she was ready to disembark. Mr. Stonewell gave final instructions to observe an report and the floor bay opened in the middle of the hull. The doors swung down giving the occupants access to make their exit. The metal bars above their heads with their harness cables attached swung up the aircraft ceiling with a quiet hum of a motor. The bars met in the middle of the hull and locked into place with the cables dangling down in front of them. The pulley motors wound the ropes tight so that they could be lower onto the ground slowly. There was little to see below with the blinding lights of the aircraft illuminating the drop zone and dust swirling on the ground below.

One by one the group unlatched from the jump seats and dangled in the center of the hull. They pressed the button on their harness which released the rope from the pulley system lowering them to the ground. Tessa had hoped for a gradual descent, but it seemed to be a quick release and drop. Tessa waited to go last and looked to the cockpit to see Professor Green and Mr. Stonewell give her the thumbs up which was supposed to motivate her to drop. It didn't do much of what they were expecting. She was slow to move but once she had let go of the jump seat and was left dangling in the air mid-hull with the gaping hole in the floor she was quick to press the button. She was grateful the descending process was fast, so she had little time to panic.

Tessa hit the ground hard, and the force nearly knocked the wind from her lungs, but adrenaline was coursing through her veins and overloading any sense of pain for the moment. She was just glad to be on solid ground once again. The aircraft retracted the ropes and then flew off to keep an eye on the perimeter. The helo left the team on the ground, and the team double-checked comms before they moved forward.

High chain-link fencing surrounded the compound with razor wire just like a prison. It made Tessa understand why the rebels believed something important might be here. There was a guard tower, but it didn't seem to be in use. It was black and silent. Her goggles picked up no movement in the towers or on the ground. The main building was a single story white concrete warehouse with no windows and only one main entrance. A digitally encrypted door lock panel to the left of the thick steel door secured the entry. Finn made short work of manipulating the lock. He mentally decrypted the lock, and the door swung open without tripping any alarms. Tessa could see why Mr. Stonewell found his abilities so desirable, but she still questioned what he wanted with hers.

The team entered one at a time, covering each other in turn as they moved through the building sweeping the rooms as they advanced. The searched through half the building consisting of empty offices without running into anyone. It looked like the H.I.V.E had evacuated this base in a hurry. The offices appeared ransacked and disheveled, and they didn't leave behind any critical documentation. They reached a door at the end of the corridor which was also digitally locked. This one took Finn a little longer to decode, but he still managed to gain entry in an impressive amount of time. On the other side, they discovered a vast laboratory. The sterile and stark white lab contained about a dozen scientists in white lab coats and safety glasses. The team drew weapons and demanded the scientist's to shelter in a corner and submit to being restrained with plastic zip-tie cuffs. Tessa and Finn refrained from participating in pulling weapons on the scientists; they only watched the scene unfold. Both hoped to remain uninvolved with any mission combat.

Vanessa volunteered to remain behind to guard the scientists as the others moved forward to examine the lab. As Tessa evaluated the room closer, it seemed like they were packing up the lab facility to evacuate as well. That would certainly explain why they didn't run into much opposition outside the building. Group chatter on the comms seemed to agree with the hypothesis. The team speculated that the facility must have become aware that the rebels discovered their location. Finn located the nearest computer terminal and began uploading data to his machines back at the base for later review.

Tessa and Melanie took their time searching the rest of the lab, but there was little left to explore. Tessa figured they had lost out on an opportunity to discover the function of the H.I.V.E facility. The two girls exited the lab space and into a cargo docking area to the back of the building. There was still one truck backed into the loading bay, and Tessa could feel energy swirling inside the semi-trailer. She was still getting familiar with her new Evo powers, but there was no denying that there was an energy signal coming from inside the trailer. The two approached the trailer door to find it locked with a thick padlock.

"Hold on I think I have the key," Tessa grabbed the lock and used her strength to tear it off the trailer door. She might not have the same finesse as Finn, but she could still get the job done. Melaine chuckled at her sarcasm.

Tessa opened the doors, and Melanie shone her flashlight into the trailer. Few words could describe what they saw inside. There were rows of upright tables with harnesses that held people strapped to them. These captive people were young men and women, and they were not cognizant. They were in some form of stasis with tubes and wires connected to their bodies. It was eerie and disturbing to see these nearly naked bodies suspended in silence wired into computers monitoring vials. Cables attached to monitors reading heart, lung, and brain function. The tubes were to feed the body and extract fluid.

"Luca!" Melanie shouted, and Tessa could sense her distress.

Tessa rounded the corner to find Melanie fumbling with one of the bodies, "Melanie, don't! We have no idea what all this is and if we can remove them without hurting or worse killing them." She put her hands on Melanie's wrists to prevent her from damaging the young man.

Melanie was crying to the point of hyperventilation "It's my brother Luca."

Tessa took only a few moments to process the scene, "This is your brother?" Melanie nodded in affirmation as she sobbed uncontrollably. "Your brother the Evo who was taken by the H.I.V.E?" Same nodding. "Don't do anything. We are going to help him alright, but we have to be careful."

Tessa led a reluctant Melanie out of the truck and found her a seat in the docking bay. Tessa had to keep her away from the trailer for fear that she might do something rash to save her brother. She stepped away from the distraught woman to a safe distance beyond earshot. Tessa kept a watchful eye on Melanie as she used the comms reaching out to Finn, "Finn we have a situation at the far end of the laboratory that exits to the cargo bay."

He was working through computer files, "Hmm...a what did you say?"

"We have a situation, and it needs attention sooner rather than later. I need you here, now."

"Let me just finish up and..."

"Now Finn!"

He paused, and a concerned voice returned to the comms, "Alright, I'm on my way. Are you okay?"

Finn burst into the cargo bay thinking that some terrible battle was about to ensue, but he slowed to a screeching halt when he saw a weeping Melanie. Tessa led him to the semi-trailer and showed him the contents along with the reason for Melanie's tears. He studied the computer outputs and concluded that all of the occupants were in fact in a medically induced stasis coma, but their minds seemed to be plugged into a virtual world to stimulate their minds making them less resistant to the stasis. Finn concluded that he had never seen anything like it before. He was afraid if he attempted to unwire their trapped minds from the matrix, it could cause serious and permanent psychosomatic damage and in a worse case scenario death. He went further to explain that if they had been sedentary for an extended period they may be unable to walk on their own and there were too many of them for the group to move.

"So what do we do? We can't leave there here?"

"No, we absolutely cannot. These are Evo experiments, and I'm not leaving fellow Evos to this fate."

"So what do we do?"

"We're taking the truck."

Finn sent word over the comms explaining what happened and the current plan to extract the Evos to safety. Stonewell volunteered to drive the truck, and Melanie refused to leave her brother. The rest of the team would accompany the truck via air support back to base. The bird circled back around to drop off Stonewell, and Finn drove the truck from the bay out into the open compound, and that was when everything went sideways.

15

As Finn drove the truck away from the docking bay, Tessa heard a loud boom accompanied by a flash of light which crossed the sky just outside the compound gates. The pulse of light made contact with something in the air near the compound. Tessa craned her neck out the passenger window to get a visual. She called out on the comms for confirmation, but the sound of dead silence was all she could hear. The truck engine died, and they both climbed out to see what caused the disturbance. Finn immediately sensed that the blast was an EMP and which targeted their aircraft with Green and Stonewell aboard.

Tessa noticed two H.I.V.E hover birds in the air and their Evo aircraft that was now dark and plummeting to the ground. Tessa ran to the open area just outside the cargo dock and time seemed to slow to a crawl as she watched their craft spiral in a freefall toward its doom. She had little time to react but made a choice to stand her ground and focused on accessing her energy power. Finn joined her and held out a hand toward the falling craft in a desperate attempt to kick start the engine with his Evo abilities. Tessa tried to supply him with the raw energy he needed to jump-start the engine, but there was not enough time. She had to make a quick decision.

Tessa thrust both of her palms out toward the craft and focused all of her energy as she had with the apple. Only this time she was trying to levitate a massive aircraft instead of a tiny apple. Her signature purple glowing surrounded the aircraft, and she could feel its weight pushing back against her energy. Tessa was determined to hold fast despite the crushing weight of the falling craft. She had superhuman strength, and she called on that power to sustain her position. Tessa couldn't stop the aircraft's decent, but she could slow it enough and stabilize it preventing it from spiraling out of control. She managed to slide the aircraft to the ground in a less violent crash than it would have been otherwise. The earth beneath it upheaved and dust flew into the air. She wasn't sure if the craft would be operational after the landing, but she was confident that the occupants had touched down unscathed.

Tessa's legs wobbled, and she lost her balance falling to her knees in the gravel. Finn grabbed her arm and pulled her back into the passenger seat of the semi-truck. Tessa wiped the bottom of her nose with the back of her right hand and examined the blood smeared on her skin. Her head pulsed in anger and she felt dizzy and nauseous. Her brain was foggy and her body tired, but she held on to consciousness and the contents of her stomach.

Finn managed to restart the truck and move it outside the cargo area and behind some buildings for cover. He parked it as close to the downed aircraft as possible. Vanessa and Melanie were waiting for the semi to arrive and they collected themselves against a concrete building wall. Protected from enemy fire, they had a clear line of sight to the aircraft. The speedster appeared from around the corner to give them a report on the enemy. Since the comms were temporarily down, it was their only means of communication. Tessa managed to pay attention to most of the conversation, but she was struggling to remain coherent. H.I.V.E was putting boots on the ground and advancing on the compound.

Stonewell burst from the back of the aircraft ready to fight. His skin seemed to have turned to stone and bullets only ricocheted off the surface. He retrieved some scrap metal and concrete pylons to create some cover near the damaged aircraft. He carried the enormous materials over his shoulder with ease. He needed Finn to get close enough to repair the airship. The team moved under cover of one another's suppressive fire to the makeshift fortifications surrounding their aircraft.

Finn used his power to remove the outer plates of the craft to reveal the damaged interior workings. He instructed the speedster he required specific parts from the enemy aircraft. The speedster braced Finn's neck in anticipation of the extreme change in velocity to avoid whiplash. The rest of the team returned fire to hold back the enemy, and Stonewell rampaged out in the open throwing massive objects at the advancing soldiers.

When Finn and Derik returned with the parts in hand, Finn began working immediately on the repairs.

Vanessa pulled massive vines from the earth and intertwined H.I.V.E agents immobilizing them in her tangled botanical web. She could use the vines to lift them from the ground and beat their entire bodies against the ground or into buildings. She could also squeeze them, but other soldiers quickly came to their rescue cutting down the vines and freeing their comrades. Gale Force challenged the helos with strong winds and lightning bolts. Even with all their team's Evo power, they were slowly losing the battle. They were trapped with no mean of escape unless Finn could repair the aircraft.

Bullets kept on coming from the air and the ground. Two of the helos were now on the ground deploying more soldiers. There were two helos still in the sky, dropping ropes to send in more infantry troops as back up. The Evo team became quickly outnumbered and outgunned.

The H.I.V.E had more advanced weapons than Tessa imagined. They used traditional assault rifles and side arms, in addition to technologically advanced weaponry which fired a blue laser light. The laser seemed to be more potent than regular bullets, and it chewed away at the concrete pylons protecting the team. If they continued firing for an extended period, the team's cover would soon be gone. The laser's still seemed ineffective on Stonewell's stone skin, but for how long could he sustain the barrage. Eventually, their sheer numbers would overwhelm him. Just when Tessa thought things couldn't get any worse, they did. H.I.V.E operatives moved in with specialized Evo weaponry. They deployed two soundwave guns on opposite sides of the speedster that stopped him dead in his tracks. They injected Vanessa's vines with a toxin that caused them to wither and die. The helo was emitting a blue light coupled with a frequency that negated Gale Force's wind powers which grounded her. Although Tessa was still dizzy from her excessive use of power, she couldn't mistake the large cannon glowing ominously red firing on Stonewell. The cannon deployed a net radiating the same color red. The weighted net entangled Stonewell and under its ominous red glow, his stone skin melted away. The net's tech had negated his power. Stonewell had no Evo armor, and he had no super strength. He struggled to break free but was failing miserably.

The comms began to crackle as Professor Green managed to get them back online. Stonewell gave an order, "Someone, get adrenaline to Tessa."

Finn replied, "No. She's barely functioning. You don't know what adrenaline could do to her."

"What choice do we have? We're pinned down here."

"Don't you dare do it!" Finn demanded.

Tessa looked up to see Vanessa hovering above her with something in her hand. She bent down to examine Tessa, "She pretty out of it."

"Do it!" Stonewell ordered.

Vanessa shoved the needle into Tessa's leg and pressed down on the syringe sending the epinephrine coursing through her veins. Finn knelt down next to her, "Tessa don't let your power consume you. Breath."

She began breathing heavy as she could feel a wave of energy building inside her body and her strength returning. The rush of adrenaline made her mind even fuzzier and as she heard the sounds of gunshots her anger grew. These people had used other human beings as experiments, and it didn't matter that they were Evos. Evos were still people. She was an Evo, and her team was in trouble trying to save these people. The only emotion she could feel was rage.

Finn tried containing her, but it was far too late to calm her now. Stonewell had done his damage and unleashed his weapon on the enemy. Tessa put on her goggles and turned on her tunes, Beastie Boys; *Sabotage* blasted in her ears. She stood slowly and with an outstretched palm a translucent purple barrier appeared in front of the team and the aircraft shielding them from fire. Tessa used the kinetic energy barrier to stop the bullets and disintegrate them upon contact. As the enemy paused in confusion, she blinked from the safety of their cover out across enemy lines. Tessa tore the net from Stonewell with her bare hands. Then she blinked to each sound gun holding the speedster and destroyed them with explosive energy.

The speedster followed her lead, and together they began a quick flurry of assaults on enemy targets before they could even comprehend what was happening. Stonewell stood his ground in front of the team and resumed throwing heavy projectiles at the larger clusters of ground soldiers in an effort break them apart into smaller more manageable groups for Tessa and Derik to pick off.

Tessa blinked to position herself under one of the helos which still had ropes dangling in the air from dropping down soldiers and also emitting the frequency dampening Gale Force's power. She reached up and wrapped one of the lines around a hand and then gave a firm tug. With her superhuman strength, it didn't take much effort for her to destabilize the helo and cause it to flounder in the sky. She tugged a little harder and sideways the second time to send it into a tailspin leading to it eventually coming to a crash landing into the compound's empty guard tower. A massive eruption of flame and explosion rocked the area. Tessa had swiftly eliminated one of their biggest threats. Stonewell focused taking out the other helo hurling an enormous chunk of concrete. Tessa aided Stonewell by charging the solid projectile with energy, and so it exploded on contact like she had the apple in Finn's shop. Then Stonewell flung projectiles at the two birds on the ground to take them out of commission. All that remained were the troops on the ground now lacking their air support.

Tessa drew her batons and blinked from place to place around the compound eliminating H.I.V.E militants. She would blink in and with a couple one two hits and a swipe of the legs she could take them down. The problem was they weren't staying down or retreating so as she blinked back to former targets. Her anger rose because of their continued hatred and their determination to bring the Evos down. They didn't just want to stop her team; these soldiers were out for blood, and so Tessa began to fight for blood. She turned to massive strength enhance blows with the batons, focusing first on blinking to take out rooftop snipers. Then she worked the soldiers on the ground leaving a trail of bodies behind.

When there were no more militants left she stopped blinking and stood disoriented in the middle of the compound chest heaving as she struggled to catch her breath after the fighting. She bent down to steady herself by placing her hands and knees on the ground to control her vertigo. She could feel her body coming down off the adrenaline surge, and she was fading fast. As she was about to lose consciousness she began to realize what she had just done. She had killed all of those men. She heard the Evo aircraft fire up. And the last thing she heard was Finn's voice running toward her as she sank into the dirt falling forward with no remaining energy.

16

Tessa hovered in and out of consciousness like an eerie out of the body experience. She could feel herself slowly regaining control of her body and as she did all the pain flooded in as well. Her head throbbed with overwhelming agony that made her stomach queasy. She found herself laying on a cot which wasn't very comfortable. She tried to peer out of squinted eyes, discovering she was in Finn's garage back at base. The fluorescent lights flooded her eyes sending sharp anguishing pain to her head making the throbbing worse.

Tessa could hear the sound of someone throwing metal tools and yelling voices. The loud noises sent more pain shooting through her head. She tried to focus on listening to her surroundings and breathed slowly to calm her stomach. "I don't care what your mission is; what you did to her was wrong, and you know it." Tessa craned her neck back to see Finn with his finger waving in Stonewell's face.

"I had a hard decision to make, and I made it. You're not responsible for everyone under this roof, and you aren't able to understand the gravity of the decisions I make every day to ensure everyone's safety."

"And what about Tessa? She didn't have a choice. You pumped her full of drugs and let her lose not knowing what would happen if she lost control. What about her safety? Is that not a concern of yours? She learned to use her powers yesterday, hours before the op. She doesn't have control yet, and you destabilized her mentally, and that's dangerous and reckless. You could have killed her or the team. You had no idea how she would react."

"Yes, I took a chance. And it worked out. We saved a dozen Evos from captive H.I.V.E experimentation. That's a win for our side no matter what angle you look at it."

"It worked this time but it was reckless, and it won't always work out Harland. She's an Alpha psionic which we can't even begin to understand her abilities.

She learned to use her power yesterday for god sake. She could have torn the whole compound down on top of us for all you know. She discovered her power, and you go and pump her up, pushing her to the edge of control. You couldn't wait to use her in combat, and that's exactly what you did, you USED her."

"I'm confident in Tessa's ability to control her power."

"Why, because you've known her for like two whole days. That's just crazy talk. Don't play me like I'm an idiot Harland. You did this because you're selfish and you'll do anything to win. Don't pretend like you even considered her well-being. As far as I'm concerned; you're no different than the H.I.V.E with their Evo experiments. That's what you did to Tessa. You experimented on her and hoped you got the desired result. I'm out. You're a lunatic pretending to care about your followers but you don't, and they're cannon fodder to you. You can't even look around to see what collateral damage you're causing."

They continued their argument as Tessa tried regaining control over her mind and body. Her vision was blurry, but she could make out that Finn was packing a truck with gear as he was yelling at Stonewell. Tessa moved her body despite stiff pain throughout her joints, but she managed to sit up. Her two human friends were at her side waiting for her to wake and they turned from the fight toward her to help her sit up. Their faces were so serious and filled with concern over her condition. They tried to ask questions about how she felt, but she was still mentally impaired.

Arica studied biology, and she looked Tessa up and down for injuries as she pleaded with her to lay back down and rest. Her hands tried to push on Tessa's shoulder to return her to the cot, but Tessa shook her away. Sam tried to help subdue her with his strength. He was in pique physical condition, but Tessa had enhanced Evo strength that was no match for either of her human friends.

Tessa looked down and noticed her hands covered in blood, and she turned them over to examine each side. She then frantically searched her body feeling for the injury and source of blood. A cruel realization set in as Tessa discovered she was not wounded. The blood on her hands wasn't hers. Her brow furled as she tried to think past the splitting headache. She struggled to remember what had happened during the mission. She slowly began to discover the frightening truth. The more she remembered, the more her hands started to shake in horror and tears began welling up in her eyes. Tessa realized what she had done, and the heaviness of truth hit her so hard she couldn't speak. All she could do was scream at her bloodstained palms. She shrieked at them in anger, struggling to come to terms with the atrocities she committed.

The room reacted in silence to her awakening. Everyone froze as they were waiting to see what she would do. She hugged herself trembling with fury; rocking back and forth on the cot. As her anger swelled, objects in the room began to vibrate. The vibrations become more violent as the sound of trembling objects intensified. What started as a dull humming, now grew to the roaring sound of metal on metal. Tools and machines vibrated to the same frequency as Tessa. She could feel the tensions in the room as she seized control of everything.

She took a long deep breath in and stood from the cot turning to face Finn and Harland. She was stone-faced and stoic. Detached from the emotion which caused the manifestation of her power. Objects in the room ceased to tremble, and they began to float illuminated by a purplish pink aura as if the rooms were devoid of gravity. She walked in confidence toward Stonewell, "What have you done to me?"

His eyes darted around the room at the floating objects, but he managed to answer, "I chose to save the team."

Tessa's eye twitched, "You decided to use me as a weapon."

He put up a hand to her, "Now wait. That's a harsh way to put it, Tessa. We were in a bind, and I had no other choice."

"I told you I only wanted to observe. There was a choice. You could have asked for my help."

"Now wait a minute. You stepped in of your own free will to prevent the hovercraft from crashing."

She was almost faced to face with him, "I wish I would have let it crash and burn with you inside." Her words were cold and calculated.

Stonewell flinched and reacted the only way he thought he could, "I'm sorry Tessa. I needed you to act for us to escape with our lives and those of the Evo prisoners."

"Finn is right. You're no different than them." She turned from him to walk away.

"This isn't the first time you've killed Tessa," he taunted her.

Tessa snapped back around to face Stonewell toe to toe. "True, but my actions were always my choice. You clouded my judgment and manipulated me." She turned her back again and walked away.

Stonewell opened his mouth in anger, "I made you."

Tessa blinked from where she was standing to directly in front of him. She wrapped a hand around his neck picking him up off his feet with the use of her strength. His skin transformed to stone in defense, but the stone began to crack under the weight of her crushing grip. Tessa screamed into his face, "You made me a monster." She tossed him across the room slamming him into the side of an armored Humvee. She moved toward him again, "You made me alright, you made me a cold-blooded killer! Did you think I would be your weapon? Your Alpha puppet?"

He stood up, "They will come for your Alpha powers. They will harvest your DNA to make weapons more powerful than any others. Then no Evo will be safe from them."

"I pity whoever comes for me. Including you."

Finn stepped between the two feuding Evos, "Tessa, don't become what he wants you to. Don't let him win. He's not worth it. Walk away." She looked at him and paused, "Leave with me," he held out an inviting hand.

Tessa declined to take his hand, but she did agree to end her assault on Stonewell. She turned away and all the floating objects came crashing to the floor as if she had turned the gravity in the room back on. She washed her hands in a shop sink and ran her fingers through her hair. She took another calming breath to reassure her new composure. She snatched up her backpack near the cot with some of her belongings inside. She was still in her jumpsuit armor and armed with her weapons, but she didn't care at this point. She didn't even bother to get the rest of her things from their room. She selected a motorcycle from several that Finn had in the shop.

Finn was next to her, "Where will you go."

"Away from this awful place. How about you?"

"I'm head east to the Appalachian Mountains."

"I've heard there's nothing left there."

"Exactly. I want to be alone. I've heard there might be some Evos hiding there. Trying to live a peaceful life."

Tessa smiled, "That sounds nice."

"So come with me."

"I'd love to, but I can't right now. I have to go home."

"They know who you are now. The H.I.V.E will come for you and they will send an army to do it."

"Let them come. I have to say goodbye to my family."

"I understand." He put a sat phone in her palm, "When you're ready, come find me."

She nodded in affirmation and then kick-started the engine. Finn activated the garage door lift with a flick of his wrist, tapping into his technopathic powers. Tessa left the base in haste and never looked back. She rode hard out of the city refusing to let Mr. Stonewell win his war of manipulation. Part of her was grateful that he had allowed her to use his resources to discover her powers. The other part of her wished that none of it had ever happened. She had left her friends behind with Professor Green but was confident that he would see them safely home. Tessa hoped that the rebels would leave her friends alone in the future. She needed this ride to clear her head and was no longer fearful of any bandits she might run into along the road home. With her powers, she felt sorry for anyone who tried to ambush her. Tessa was already fuming mad and now a murderer. She had killed before but only for survival. This time was different, she was killing in the name of someone else, and she had no desire to be a puppet. A few more victims were trivial at this point, especially if they were the bandits asking for trouble.

Tessa already hated herself because of her new Evo blood, but now she loathed herself on a whole new level. She was a monster. A force who could take lives, which had already taken lives. Someone dangerous. She knew that at some point she would face the decision to either kill or be killed. Stonewell had taken away that free will by pumping her full of adrenaline to erode her mental control. He manipulated her into becoming his killer. She never wanted anyone on the team to die. If Tessa had her rational mind, she could have figured a way for them to escape without a murderous rampage. It wasn't right that Stonewell took that decision from her.

The H.I.V.E would run facial recognition software until they knew her identity. It wouldn't take long before they discovered her family and showed up on their doorstep looking for her. She hoped that she could return home long enough for a short explanation and to say her goodbyes. After that, she wasn't sure what to do with her life. Tessa knew she had to disappear but was she better off alone or could she stay with Finn. He didn't seem to want to exploit her. But if there were other Evos, how could she be sure it was safe? Rebels and H.I.V.E alike might come back to the mountains in search of hidden Evos.

As Tessa rocketed home at full speed, the weight of her new future seemed to crush her spirits. She realized how alone she was. Tessa was an Evo; who the human world shunned. She was an Alpha Evo; a freak even in the Evo world. She didn't feel as though she belonged in either world. Now hunted for being different, H.I.V.E would want her head as a trophy and Evos would want her to fight. There was no peace for her unless she could exist alone.

17

Tessa rode long and hard throughout the day with the harsh sun bearing down on her in the open plains. Living in this wasteland; she had become accustomed to the unrelenting rays that caused this world so much pain and anguish. The sun dried up crops and turned wind to dust storms that ravaged the land. She wished she could turn back time and warn humanity to stop the abuse and to care for nature before it was too late. If humankind had known how terrible things would turn out, they might have made different choices.

As Tessa came closer to Stillwater, she began to exit the recesses of her mind. She turned her focus outward toward her surroundings searching the horizon for any rising threats. If the military had captured her face to discover her identity, they could be lurking nearby awaiting her return home. She had to stay vigilant. She knew that it was only a matter of time before they discovered her. Tessa needed just a few precious moments to see her family one last time before she left them forever. She had to abandon everything that she had grown to love and leave it behind for a life of solitude and hopefully peace. She figured this world's days were numbered anyway. Regardless of what either side accomplished this world was doomed to fail. She could only hope for a few good years of happiness and calm before mother nature decided to turn on humanity and wipe the species from existence.

Tessa wondered if the Evos might survive a little longer than humans. They were after all more evolutionary advanced, but they were still human at their core. She wished that humankind could see that they needed each other. Humans and Evos alike are necessary to work together and survive this world. The division and fighting would be their ultimate undoing. It seemed impossible to convince either side to cooperate. They had both dug in their heels and decided that their path was the righteous one and they refused to entertain any ideals that weren't their own. Humanity was so embroiled in conflict and hate. They were incapable of looking past their selfish desires. They failed to notice that they were killing civilization with their sheer will to disagree. Humanity loved violence and turmoil. There was a long history to prove it as fact.

That had been the way of their entire civilization. War and destruction were what made the world turn. The rise and fall of regime. The cult of personality and the unwavering urge to follow the crowd like a herd with one collective mind. Religious debates and political animosity fueled the world since the beginning of humankind on the planet. Humanity had sabotaged its own existence throughout time and revealed in the torture and exploitation of those perceived as weaker. Tessa was surprised that mother earth had let them ravage her for so long. It was only a matter of time before humankind imploded and mother reclaimed her planet. It seemed like there was no way to prevent or detour humanity from this destructive path. The damage is already done, with no reversal course of action in sight. Tessa would watch the end of the world from her quiet corner and laugh as they are all devoured by their own hate. Death would come for everyone regardless of whose side they supported.

Tessa rode up to the farmhouse as dusk was falling on the outstretched fields. She took a few moments to watch the sunset as it fell over the horizon. The beautiful colors of purple, orange, and pink painted the sky, and the clouds softened the picturesque view. She may never gaze on these fields again. Tessa always wanted to remember this spot where she grew up. The home where she learned about the world; back when everything seemed innocent before she had become jaded by the politics and selfishness of humanity. There was something serene about the simplicity of nature. Even though it appeared hostile, nature was an unwavering constant. It was, what it was. There was no hidden agenda or lies; just being.

Tessa kept a watchful eye as she parked the bike and walked up the porch steps of her childhood home. Evie was on the living room floor watching the television with her father. He concentrated on cleaning out some old gunked up machine parts with a shop towel. Mother hated when he piled up all those nasty parts on the end table. There was too much work to do, and he often brought work inside so he could enjoy his family while continuing to work. There were not enough hours in the day to get all the work done to keep the farm sustainable. People were counting on these crops to survive, and father wanted to do his part. With Tessa gone, there would be more work on his plate and less time to spend with family.

Tessa was so quiet when she entered that no one stirred in the living room. She watched as if her family were a picture on the television and she was the audience observing them. Tessa tried to freeze this moment in time inside her mind. Evie sprawled out on her stomach kicking her legs back and forth in the air in a cotton gingham dress. Chin in her palms propped up by her elbows. Shifting her head side to side with blond pigtails swaying to and fro. Evie was the last picture of innocence Tessa would ever see. Evie had turned six not long ago and remained untainted by the realities of this world. Nothing would ever be the same again. This place would never again be her home.

Tessa's brother, Andy bound down the staircase and into the foyer nearly on top of her. "Tessa, I almost didn't recognize you. Welcome home." He patted her on the back and headed to the kitchen. Upon her announcement, Evie perked up with offerings of hugs for her older sister. She was the only one in the family that knew the truth. Evie knew what her sister was, but Tessa dared not add murderer to the list of secrets of which she was aware. That would be a secret she planned on taking to the grave.

Tessa's mother came out of the kitchen with a dish towel drying her hands, "Tessa, we weren't expecting you home today."

"Well plans changed unexpectedly." Tessa nodded to her father as she made her way to the kitchen.

"Well sit down. I'll set a place for you at the table. There's plenty of food. We can share." Her mother smiled, and Tessa's heart broke into a million pieces. She looked down at Evie and back to her mother. This situation was one of the hardest moments of her life. She had thought it was the moment she discovered she was an Evo. Or even the moment that she cheated her way out of the government-supervised Evo test. She was wrong. Nothing compared to the weight of this moment.

Her mom could tell something was wrong, "Tessa, what's a matter?" She paused and focused on her child, "Why are you dressed like that?"

Tessa realized that she was still in her armor and with weapons and all. She looked down shrugged and looked back to her mom, "Things have changed. I wasn't at a school convention."

"Where were you?" She was starting to get upset putting her hands on her hips ready to unleash motherly justice. Tessa would have accepted any punishment her mother could dish out if she could avoid what she knew was inevitable.

"You should sit down." Tessa joined her mom and Evie at the kitchen table. "I was in Kansas City, at the rebel base."

"What! Why on earth would you go there?" The outburst prompted her father and brother to join the conversation at the kitchen table.

"Look this is going to be hard for you to understand. Evie, you can help me." She smiled at her sweet little sister. "On the day of the Evo attack at school, my life changed. It wasn't like what you might have heard. My Evo abilities manifested that day, and that's the truth. The rebels helped me hide it from the H.I.V.E investigators that came to the school but only if I agreed to visit their base. So I did, and that's where I've been. I'm in trouble now with both sides, and I don't want anything to do with either. All I ever wanted was to live here with all of you under this roof. But I can't now. I have to run. I've come to say goodbye." Tears were rolling down her cheeks, and she could see the same of her mother and Evie. The boys were trying to stay strong.

"Are you sure?" Her brother didn't want to believe what she was. Her father was thinking the same, but he remained silent.

"I'm sure." She levitated all the place settings above the kitchen table, making things more awkward.

Her mother took a deep breath, "I don't care you're still my daughter." She leaned in toward Tessa pulling her in for a hug, "I knew it was bound to happen somewhere down the line. We do have Evo blood in our family tree."

Tessa had never known that family secret, but that wasn't something most people liked to talk about, "Who?"

"My sister. They took her when she tested at sixteen."

"What were her abilities?"

"Don't know. We never got a chance to say goodbye."

Her father nervously spoke, "We shouldn't be talking about this."

"It's not going to go away dad. Not talking about it doesn't change a thing."

Her mother defended her, "This is our daughter, and she's always safe here."

Tessa shook her head, "No. I'm not safe anywhere. And you are all not safe with me around."

As if on cue, she could hear the faint whipping of helicopters and the sound of tires on gravel. They were here for her, and she was out of time. Everyone at the table knew it too. She tried to herd them all into the safety of the basement, but she only managed to get her brother and sister to obey. Her mother was not going to let them take her baby, and her father wasn't going to allow anything to happen to the farm or his family. It was a no-win situation for them. Tessa knew there was an arsenal outside awaiting her. The H.I.V.E had already seen what she was capable of and she was sure they had taken precautions. They knew she was there and had the farmhouse surrounded.

Tessa moved to the front door in an attempt to remove her family from harm. She exited the door to find it now dark outside, and a cluster of bright lights focused in on her. She felt like she was stepping onto a stage, the spotlight blinding her with flooding light. She held her arm up to shield her eyes, but no matter how hard she squinted she could not see beyond the lights. This circumstance was a spot she had no desire to be stuck. She stepped off the porch to assess her situation and examine her options for escape.

A woman's voice blared over a bullhorn, "Tessa Jones, put your hands up and get down on the ground.

We do not wish to take you by force, but we will do whatever is necessary to ensure your compliance. You are a danger to those around you and must be removed from society. We would prefer to do this peacefully."

Tessa started to put her hands up when she heard the farmhouse screen door slam behind her. Before she could glance behind to see what was happening, she heard a single gunshot echo through the air. Tessa turned to find Evie standing frozen on the sidewalk below the porch. She had a pearl necklace in her hand and a frightened look on her face. Tessa witnessed a dark red blood stain growing in the center of her chest. Tessa used her Evo ability and blinked from her location to catch her sister as she fell to the ground gasping for air.

As she caught Evie, she heard another shot and then felt a pain in the back of her neck. She ignored it and held her dying sister tight. Her mother came off the porch screaming, and her father started cursing at the lights. Tessa took the now blood-soaked pearls from Evie and kissed the back of her hand as her life slipped away. She watched in agony as her baby sister took her final breath and her mother slipped into a state of maternal madness.

Tessa could feel that rage building up inside her again as it had before. This time it was different. This time it was stronger. She laid Evie's head down in the grass and stood clutching the pearls in one hand. She squeezed them hard and reached for the source of pain in the back of her neck. She found a tranquilizer dart and pulled it from her skin throwing it to the ground. She could hear the enemy ready their weapons. They best be prepared for what she was about to unleash.

Tessa could feel the tranquilizer drugs coursing through her body, and she struggled to maintain control of her motor functions. It was working its magic to subdue her, and it would eventually win. They wanted her alive so they could exploit her power, and they would gun down anyone who threatened to stand in their way. But for now, she had a few precious minutes to wreak havoc on them and dispense justice. Not justice, vengeance. She could have taken what little time she had left to run, but she didn't want to run right now. She wanted to murder every last one of these assholes she could get her hands on and more. She wanted retribution for Evie. Evie was young and innocent. They would pay for what they had done today. Tessa would see them all die for this. She would avenge her sister.

Everything around Tessa started to glow purple as she harnessed every last bit of energy she could muster. She began to pull everything piece of H.I.V.E equipment apart with a seething fury. She dismantled guns and vehicles tearing them apart piece by piece, and exploding them in a massive burst of energy combustion. She felt another stinging tranq dart but continued her rampage. Another and she began slowing to a crawl and started to losing hold of her power. She slumped to the ground, and the world started to spin. She fell face first into the grass, and everything went black.

18

Tessa began to stir as she started to awaken, opening her eyes to bright fluorescent lighting. Her head pounded as she squinted around trying to discover where she was. Tesa found herself lying in a hospital bed with an IV in her arm and hooked to monitor screens displaying her vitals. She moved slowing trying to roll herself out of bed. She figured she would have been tied down but was shocked discovering that she was free. So she planted her bare feet on the cold tile floor and attempted to stand.

Tessa was weak and wobbled as she tried to gain her balance. She grabbed the monitors on a wheeled pole with IV fluids and rolled it toward the door trying to see if anyone was around to notice her revival. She didn't hear or see anyone so she began inspecting the IV in her arm, trying to figure out a way to remove it so she could make a break for it.

Two male nurses entered the room to find her up and moving and tried to coax her into returning to the bed. They knew her name and seemed polite in asking rather than the forceful demands she was anticipating. Tessa tried to harness her power and use it to push them away, but there was nothing. No power available to be seized. Confused by her failure, she was pulled back toward the bed engaged in a verbal argument with orderlies.

She stopped short when she saw her mother enter the room, "Mom?"

"Gentlemen, please. Leave us. I'll see that she's alright." The orderlies left the room as instructed and her mother continued, "I'm so sorry Tessa. Please have a seat."

"Mom, where are we?" Tessa sat back down on the bed.

"I think you got a pretty big jolt if you think I'm your mother."

"What are you talking about?"

"I'm Norine, your mother's twin sister."

"The Evo?"

"Evo?   What in the world are you talking about?"

"Mom said you were an Evo and they took you at sixteen."

"Tessa you're scaring me. Do you not remember me? Do you not remember that we work here together as scientists in the H.I.V.E?"

"Scientists? The H.I.V.E?" Tessa looked around even more confused. Was she in the H.I.V.E right now? That was a terrifying notion.

"Tessa you've been here for months working with Tesla coils, and you got a pretty big jolt the other day. I'd say it's messed with your wiring a bit. Let me get the doctor."

She walked over to the door and pressed a call button. Tessa's mind was racing in a million different directions. She had no idea what was going on, but something seemed off. She couldn't have imagined everything. This place couldn't be real. Or maybe it was.

The doctor came in, but Tessa remained skeptical, "Tessa, good to see you awake. How are we feeling?"

"Confused." He looked back to Norine and then back to her as he shined a light in her eyes and checked her heart with the stethoscope.

"Confused? Explain, what are you so confused about?"

"None of this is familiar. I've never been here, and I didn't know my mother had a twin."

"Who Norine? You've been working together for months."

"That's what she says, but that's not what I remember."

"What do you remember?"

"I'm an Evo."

He chuckled, "Tessa I can promise you that there isn't a drop of Evo blood in your body. You're here working as a scientist."

"And my family?"

"Back home on the fields of Oklahoma I suppose." He looked to Norine, and she confirmed.

"So why can't I remember any of this?"

"Well, you received a nasty jolt of electricity from one of the Tesla coils you were working on, so it seems to have caused a bout of amnesia."

"Amnesia?"

"Acute. You still remember your family in Oklahoma, so it hasn't affected long-term memory. Only the short term. I suspect it's only temporary and you should regain your memories in a few weeks."

"A few weeks?"

"Yes, and in the meantime, you need to take it easy and get plenty of rest. Be sure to take all of you prescribed medicine and that should help cut down that time frame." He handed her a blue pill and a glass of water. Then he returned to the computer monitor to type his prognosis before leaving her in the room with Norine to take her meds. It made Tessa uneasy to look at Norine. She looked too much like her mother, and it was hard for her to process.

As the doctor was getting ready to leave Arica came into the room overjoyed to see her friend awake.

She hugged Tessa, "I'm so glad you're alright. You gave us all such a scare."

Arica's presence was even more confusing than Norine's, but it made her feel better about the whole situation. If Arica was here and had been here with her, then she must have been here all along. Could all of her recent memories be nothing but a bad dream? The dreams seemed so real, but so did all of this. She could feel the pain of the IV in her arm. But she had felt the pain of the tranq darts too. She took the blue pill hoping that it would calm her nerves. It wore her out just thinking about what might be her actual reality.

Norine eventually returned to work promising to revisit Tessa later that evening, but Arica showed up as she left. Tessa gently probed her friend, and Arica answered all of the questions confidently and without hesitation. Tessa didn't think she was lying. What reason would Arica have to lie to her? It seemed like they had been here and working together the whole time. She was starting to believe that her Evo powers and her stay with the rebels were nothing but a vivid dream. The mind was a powerful muscle. It was capable of manifesting all kinds of memories or imagination and a high voltage dose of electricity could have altered the synapses in her brain. She would have to give it the few weeks and see if her memories returned.

After Arica conclude her visit, Tessa laid back down to rest. Her mind had been running nonstop since waking, and she was exhausted. She wished that she could remember all of this. It was a bizarre feeling not knowing what was a dream and what was real. This reality seemed real, and Arica was here to back that up, but there was something deep inside of her that wanted to question it. The other reality had seemed so real. She wasn't sure that the human mind was capable of creating such lifelike dreams, but if she was deep enough in her subconscious mind, she supposed that anything could be possible. Over the next few weeks, she hoped to discover the truth. For now, all she wanted to do was rest.

The next day the doctor felt she was well enough to be discharged from care. She had a follow-up appointment and care instructions to take the blue pill regularly and notify him if she noticed anything out of the ordinary. That was a hard concept since everything seemed out of the ordinary. She didn't remember where her quarters were so Arica escorted her. Arica explained that they were at the H.I.V.E base in the Cheyenne Mountain Complex that was once the site of NORAD when the United States was still in power. The mountain complex was the safest place in North America buried nearly two thousand feet inside the Cheyenne Mountain near Colorado Springs. Surrounded by the strong granite of the Rocky Mountains, the facility had state of the art engineering to protect the bunker from any manner of outside attack or natural disaster. Tessa couldn't image a safer place existing anywhere else in the world, but it was possible that some of the old nations in Europe and elsewhere also had similar type bunkers. At this point, it was every man for himself, and most of the once warring nations now focused on just surviving.

Arica led Tessa through the winding corridors and toward the heart of the base where they took an elevator down three floors to a level with several apartments. The hallways and rooms painted a stoic white, gave a feeling of clean spaces and fresh air. It was a sterile and controlled environment. At times the surroundings gave Tessa a cold feeling that sent a shiver down her spine. They passed people in the hallways. Most were scientists with their white lab coats on looking down at papers as they walked paying little attention to her and Arica. There was a few military personnel dressed in black fatigues armed with rifles and handguns. She was sure that security was tight here and that those living under the mountain lived under heavy surveillance. She knew from history lessons that most of the H.I.V.E's valuable research happened here and secrets were essential to protect. Tessa just wished she could remember what kind of secret project she was working on, but she figured it wouldn't be long before she found out.

Arica opened Tessa's door and waved her in with an inviting gesture. She slowing entered the room hoping that something inside would jog her memory. All it did was cause more confusion. There wasn't much in the place that offered any insight. It was a standard room with a simple metal framed twin bed, a desk with reading lamp and computer, television, a small sofa and a partitioned bathroom with standing shower, sink and toilet. It was sterile, same as the rest of the bunker. There was little color besides white, gray and black everything in this place seemed to be monochromatic. The lack of color seemed to depress Tessa. She wondered how she could ever manage to live in such a dull environment.

It was a small studio no more than five hundred square feet and not much bigger than her whole bedroom back on the farm. Arica apologized for the size and drab décor. She explained that everyone got the same standard room unless of course, you were higher ranking on the command chain. Tessa could hear the disappointment in her voice. She was also hoping that seeing the room might trigger some latent memory.

Tessa invited her in, and they sat on the couch as Arica tried to explain how life inside the mountain worked. Tessa found her mind shifting and barely able to focus, "What about Sam?"

"Oh, he's out training. He was drafted into the military at the same time we were assigned to the labs. He should be back in the next few weeks. He's assigned to work security here."

"What exactly am I working on here?"

She smiled, "It's fascinating. You have been assigned to work on reviewing Tesla's old theories."

"Why Tesla?"

"We are all assigned to work in a specific area. I work in biology, specifically Evo genetic mutations. You work in energy research. People are working on reviving the old systems that existed before the collapse; there's a group for solar, wind and hydro-electric power. Then there are more theoretical groups, like your group that's revisiting Tesla's theories. Do you want to visit the lab? Maybe that would help you remember if you could get back to work."

"I suppose it couldn't hurt."

Tessa took her room key from Arica, and the two took the elevator back up to the top floor to the research labs floor. They were all partitioned off into hallway corridors and each required specific badge credentials to access individual labs. Tessa didn't have her badge, so Arica rang the buzzer at the door to her assigned lab and awaited a response. There was an unlatching sound, and the two entered the lab reception area. There was a young girl at a circular white desk with a phone earpiece in, and she was finishing up a call as they entered. She held up one finger to acknowledge them as she completed the call.

"Tessa so glad to see you back. We've missed you in the lab."

Tessa looked to Arica confused, and she filled the receptionist in, "Tessa is having some memory problems since the incident."

"Oh heavens, I'm so sorry to hear that." She came from around the desk dress in a professional black sheath dress and introduced herself, "Elissa Graves, I'm your lab's secretary. If there's anything you need just ask, and I'm happy to take care of it." She was too perky for Tessa, and it was painful to listen to her voice.

"We need her badge." Arica didn't hesitate to ask.

"No problem." She walked back around the desk and rummaged through some papers, "I have Tessa's badge here and a visitor badge for your Arica." She placed a hard plastic badge with Tessa's photo on it and a plain yellow badge on top of the desk.

Arica retrieved the badges and gave Tessa hers, and they both proceeded to the air locked lab door with another security swipe. Arica swiped her badge as Tessa noticed a camera angled just above the door monitoring access to the lab. She had an eerie feeling of being watched. The camera wasn't the only reason for the feeling. The whole bunker seemed under such tight lock and key that she felt strangely claustrophobic and it wasn't just because of her tiny rooms. She felt the ominous, oppressive weight of the strict government factions weighing down on this place.

She tried the shake the uneasy feeling of being watched 24/7 and focus on the lab ahead of her. She enjoyed science at school and was eager to discover what she had been working on here in the H.I.V.E lab. She met smiling faces, none of which were familiar, and well wishes. It seemed like at least she was well liked by her colleagues. That was a different feeling for her. She had always been a bit of an outcast at school. It was odd that she would be so widely liked in this forum. She wondered what was so different here as opposed to back home.

Her Aunt Norine met her at the lab and ushered through the laboratory for a quick tour. It was different from a chem or bio lab. In fact, it was an engineering laboratory. It had a feel of research and development that made Tessa feel a little more at home. It was more like a workshop than a lab, and so it reminded her of the farm's barn or Finn's shop. She had to stop her train of thought to recourse herself because Finn's shop wasn't real. But it had popped into her mind as real as anything that was standing before here. She could remember every inch of that workshop and the details were undeniable. She either had a really active imagination, or something strange was going on.

She indulged the possibility of this reality and continued to follow her Aunt on the tour, pushing the memories or dreams whichever they were from her mind at least for the time being. She would revisit them all when she was alone and had more time to reflect on the plausibility of both realities. She found that her alleged work here was intense and fascinating. The possibility of rediscovering Tesla's original theories and testing their new applications was a fantastic idea to advance future technology.

As Norine was explaining different projects in the lab, a petite Asian woman in a lab coat made her way to Tessa. She held out an open hand, "Tessa, I'm Elegia Fang, head scientist over all engineering research and development divisions, we are pleased to see that you have returned home to your lab. I've heard of your unfortunate memory-related side effects of your accident, and I hope for a speedy recovery. You have been progressing nicely in your work. I hope we can get back on schedule quickly once your memories return. In the meantime"... she gestured to the lab secretary who was wheeling a cart heaped with books, "Miss Graves has compiled a list of reading on the subject of Tesla's work. We thought that the reading might help to kick-start the recovery of your memories."

Tessa took a few moments to glance over the books, "This is some of Tesla's lost work that was allegedly stolen from his room by the United States FBI after his death."

"We managed to recover some of the top secret documents for our former order. Many of the texts are very enlightening. You may want to start with those. They cover in great detail the subject of your experimentation with the Tesla coils which sent you to the hospital."

"I see all different types of experiments in this lab, but what exactly have I been working one."

She waved Tessa to follow, "I'll show you."

They entered a side room with another swipe of her badge and Tessa was amazed by the contents of this room. It was an expansive round room which looked even more like a shop with a high ceiling and a metal railed balcony that encircled the room. There were electrical panels embedded in the walls with gauges reading electrical input and output. Spaced out on the floor of the room were rows of Tesla coils which were massive in scale. She imagined the production from these coils was immense and she could understand how a jolt might put her in the hospital. The coils circular tops towered over them looming ominous and powerful.

Dr. Fang continued her explanation of the project, "You have been working with these coils and trying to prove Tesla's theory of Aether."

"Aether was never proven."

"Perhaps. In Tesla's book that you will re-examine, he describes having a deep connection with the Aether and explains how that force feels surrounding him. He explained the Earth itself has an energy source all around us that we can harness with minimal effort without use for fuel. Eliminating the use of fossil fuels, wind, hydro, solar or nuclear power. As you were studying his works, you described much of the same feelings as Tesla. We felt that you had a connection with the Earth's Aether, and so I assigned you to this project. You were working to use the oscillator," she pointed to the machine on the back wall, "to match the resonance frequency of the Earth so that you could tap into the Aether and power the coils. We believe you were successful and that the result was your unfortunate hospitalization and amnesia. So we are hoping for a speedy recovery to try again, this time without injury or course."

She patted Tessa's back in good faith and walked away to discuss other research projects with scientists in the lab. That left Tessa feeling even more lost than she was before. She couldn't remember anything about any of this supposed research. How could this study be such an essential part of her life and her not remember a thing? Her aunt and Arica both reassured her that with time her memories would return and reading the books would hopefully jog her memory.

Tessa and her friends left the lab, and they split off in other directions. Both Arica and Norine needed to stop by their respective lab projects, so Tessa was on her own. She knew where her quarters were and wanted to run and hide there until she could figure things out. But she stood frozen in the hallway as she reflected on everything that had happened since she awoke. This moment was her first opportunity to take in her surroundings without someone around telling her how she should think. There wasn't much in the hallway but what was there spoke volumes. The only things in the hall were a couple of cameras mounted to the ceiling. She wondered what the need for so many cameras could be. There was expensive equipment in the labs, but this place seemed like a fortress. She doubted anyone could manage to steal anything. The security here was tight so why spy on a hallway. She wondered who was behind the eye in the sky and why they were spying on everyone.

Tessa started to head in the direction of her flat, and as she rounded the hall corner, she paused and back-peddled back around the corner. She positioned herself under the camera hoping no one noticed her lurking in the hallway. It was late enough that there wasn't any traffic at that moment. She paused because she didn't expect to find her aunt still loitering in the hall. She had seemed eager to be on her way, but here she was conversing with a stoic woman in the hallway. Tessa peaked around the corner and noticed some of the woman's characteristics that lead her to believe that this woman had a significant amount of authority. She was an older woman with short nearly white platinum blond hair and dressed in a well-tailored business suit. She was well groomed, and her body language intimidated her aunt. She could see that her aunt was nervous when she was talking to his women.

Tessa listened as the woman spoke to her aunt, "How has she reacted to the situation?"

"She's confused, but she will come around."

"She seems to have many questions."

"That's natural. She has no memory of this place."

"Do you think she will comply?"

"Yes, she will do the work here. I'm confident she will perform as we need her to."

"Does she have access to feel the energy as she needs to?"

"There is a small window."

"And you can assure me that she is under control?"

"She is what we need her to be and nothing more."

The woman reached out to embrace Norine and pulled her in tight. She pressed up against her aunt and kissed her passionately on the lips. "I trust you to handle the situation as needed." She walked off down the hallway in the opposite direction, and Norine turned in the other direction.

Tessa took off toward the other end of the hallway and hurried around the corner to the lifts. She wanted the solitude of her flat. Tessa needed that sanctuary. She wasn't sure of her reality. Could it be real? How could she know it was real if she had no memory of anything? What was her Aunt supposed to make sure she did?

Once she arrived at her flat, she closed the door behind her and pressed her back to the door. She soaked up her living space that didn't seem like her space at all. She could feel a headache coming on, and she squeezed her head in her hands as she slid her back down the door and to the floor lost in her own mind. Everything about this place was convincing, but it was still off. She couldn't put her finger on it, but something was wrong. Her other reality that she did remember seemed more real, but the doctor here called it nothing more than a vivid dream. She had never known her imagination to be so graphic and lifelike. It felt so real. Could it have been a dream?

She moved to the bed in hopes of getting some sleep but the rest she sought never came. Questions and doubt swirled in her mind preventing her from sleeping. Tessa reluctantly turned to the Tesla books delivered to her room. Maybe the doctors and her friends were right, perhaps the contents of these books would jog her memory.

19

Tessa buried herself in the Tesla books as a desperate attempt to regain some of her memories. The text was interesting but didn't answer any of her profound questions. The books served as more of a welcomed distraction from her own wandering mind. Tessa's thoughts were all over the place, and she couldn't sleep when her brain was so active. If she laid down and closed her eyes, all she managed to accomplish was dwell on all the mysteries she had at the moment, and that left a mountain of questions with no answers. These concerns continued to pile up in her mind and since she couldn't come to any definite conclusions every manner of potential scenario flooding through her mind. Every what if situation poured through her on a continuous loop stressing her out more and more by the minute.

Tessa managed to occupy herself well into the early hours of the morning, and eventually, her eyes became heavy enough that she might be able to get some rest. She lazily pushed the books aside on the bed making just enough room for her to curl up and lay down. She didn't mind sharing the space with all the books. She was much too tired now and putting away the books seemed beyond her energy level at the moment. She wanted to capitalize on this fleeting moment and grab what sleep she could while her mind allowed her the luxury.

Tessa dozed off, and her mind slipped deep into REM sleep, and there the dreams began to flow. But they didn't feel like dreams; they felt real. In her dream, Tessa wielded a great power against a foe. She couldn't make out who she was fighting as light flooded her vision preventing her from seeing a face. Tessa could hear the faint sounds of helicopters and a voice shouting into a bullhorn. She couldn't make out what they were saying, but she could tell by their tone of voice that they were angry. It was like she was reliving this moment in slow motion.

Tessa felt like she was floating in an out of body experience. She could feel herself moving but had no control of her body. She turned to look behind her to see a young girl with a gingham dress and blond pigtails running toward her. She couldn't have been more than six years old. A loud shot rang out, and the child fell. Tessa rushed to catch her as she was falling and a wave of emotional pain washed over her. The child was shot, and blood began pouring from the wound. Rage filled Tessa's heart, and tears filled her eyes. With outstretched hands toward the menacing lights, a powerful purple light crept over her hands, and that light tore everything apart in her wake.

Tessa awoke in a panic sitting up straight in bed drenched in sweat and screaming. She was breathing hard and crying hysterically. Evie, she remembered Evie's death. Was it real? Or was it just a bad dream? It felt real. Her scream had caught someone's attention, and a medical team came bursting through her door. They immediately started looking her over and trying to calm her down. She was still in shock from the dream, and she fought them only a little. More because their intrusion had startled her than her not wanting to cooperate. They hooked her up to a machine to monitor her heart rate and blood pressure. It seemed like both were through the roof.

After a few minutes on the machine, the orderlies were successful in calming her down, and a doctor strolled into the room. He wasn't the same doctor from earlier, but he seemed to be versed in her condition. He looked at a chart and back to her, "Tessa, tell me what happened?"

"I don't know. It was just a bad dream I guess. A nightmare."

"What was it about?"

"Hard to say, I don't remember much," she lied. Tessa remembered all of it but just wasn't sure if it was a dream or if it was real. If it was real, then these people were trying to hide the truth from her, and she didn't want them to know the questions she had about these foggy memories. It was best she kept that to herself until she knew more. If they were lying to her about this then what else were they lying to her about?

The doctor scribbled in his notebook, "You seem to be calming down. He pulled a container of pills out of his lab coat and shook two pills into his palm to offer her. "Take a couple of these to calm your nerves." He left the room to get a glass of water for her bathroom tap. He returned to hand her the glass, "Do you think they were residual memories returning?"

Tessa was suspicious of the question. He was trying to seem nonchalant, but she could tell he was nervous about something. "I doubt it." When he turned around, she glanced at the orderlies who were distracted packing up the monitoring equipment. She looked down at the pills in her hand. They seemed innocent, but she was beginning to doubt they were. She pocketed the pills and took a sip of the water pretending to swallow the pills.

The doctor finished his write up, bid her good evening, and then excused himself from the room. Tessa was alone again in this foreign place more confused than she was before. She pulled the pills from her pocket. There was something wrong with this place. There was something wrong with her. None of this felt right. She didn't feel like this was her truth, the dream had seemed more real. Those emotions were real and raw. But if her dream was real, then Evie was dead. She didn't want that to be true.

Tessa needed to discover what was real and what was false. There was one thing she was dying to know. Did she have the abilities that she used in the dream? Was she an Evo? She crossed her legs in front of her on the bed and tried to relax her mind. She concentrated on her breathing; in through the nose and out through the mouth. She reached back into the recesses of her mind to see if anything extraordinary was there lurking in the shadows. It was odd. There was a strange feeling floating there in her mind, like a fog. There was something in her mind polluting her thoughts. The fog was blocking her from connecting with something, from reaching something she could fell hiding just behind. What was it protecting?

She concentrated harder and pushed through it toward the other side. Was it the truth? She could feel power there beyond her reach. Tessa opened her eyes and scanned the room for something to test out the power. She needed to start small. She found a pen on her writing desk and focused all of her thoughts on the pen. She felt some sharp pains in her temples as she struggled to push past whatever was blocking her from the power. After some time and a headache, she managed to reach her power and stir the pen. It shook violently on the table. She concentrated harder on the pen, and it lifted from the table and flew across the room into her hands.

Tessa sprung from the bed in her eureka moment. This place was the lie. Her dreams were the reality. The realization was liberating but then, unfortunately, opened the door for a new list of puzzles. She wasn't sure she was safe here. Norine was definitely her mother's twin; there was no mistaking that, but did she have Tessa's best interests in mind. She had to question her aunt's motives, and everyone else's for that matter. She wondered what Arica might know or if she was part of this ruse. How could they keep her power and her memories from her?

Tessa wondered what this place actually was. It was the source of their government but what were they doing here? With all the ongoing research considered, they had to be up to something. Tessa needed to figure out what was going on and why. And then she needed to escape, sooner rather than later. She was itching to go, now wondering how dangerous this place was for her. She was an Evo in the heart of the H.I.V.E, but they were treating her like a human and seemed to be suppressing her power somehow. Why would they do this?

The anxiety was killing her, and she needed to talk about this with someone. Tessa decided to make the trek to Arica's room and see what she thought of these new developments. She was risking exposing herself, but she and Arica had been friends since childhood. Tessa refused to believe that Arica would betray her. The real trick was making it to her room without attracting too much attention, especially after her freak out. It was early enough in the morning that people were awake and moving around preparing for their day and reporting to their respected posts. Tessa had a sneaking suspicion that she was a target of interest and the eye in the sky would keep a close eye on her.

Tessa straightened her clothes and hair. She was in a hurry and didn't want to change. All the outfits in her closet were the same, so it didn't matter which one she wore. She just smoothed out some of the wrinkles to conceal the fact that she had slept in these clothes. Tessa strolled down the sterile white corridors and tried her best to manage a path avoiding as many cameras as possible. She would duck underneath cameras in the hope of disappearing long enough for whoever was following her to lose her location. Or at least they would have to take a few moments to find her again. Tessa had no idea what she was trying to do because she had little idea who or what she was up against. She just tried to appear as if she was casually traversing the hall on her way to her friend's flat.

Tessa arrived at Arica's flat and knocked to announce herself. It took a few moments before Arica answered. Judging from her sleepy disheveled look Tessa had woke her, but Arica let her friend inside and offered some coffee. Tessa wasn't tired; instead, she was excited about her recent discovery, but she accepted the coffee to be polite. Arica was going to need her wits for what Tessa was about to spill. Hopefully coffee would get her neurons firing.

They sat at a table and Arica yawned, "Why on earth are you up at this ungodly hour?"

"I had a nightmare." She paused unsure how exactly to explain this, "It wasn't a nightmare. It was more like uncovering the truth."

"Tessa the doctor went over all of this with you. These vivid dreams which you believe are real; they are just dreams and nothing more. When you're so deep in REM sleep like in your coma, the dreams can be strong."

"Okay I can agree with the science but what do you remember about how we got here?"

"We tested into the science division, and transferred here."

"Why would I test into the science division? Everyone knows that my strength is combat and tactics."

"You're also a brilliant engineer. You must have scored better than you thought on your science test. Besides they may have thought your engineering talents could be of use in the Tesla project."

"You know as well as I do that most of my engineering talents are highly tactical. My forte is weapons and security."

She sipped her coffee, "Who knows why the H.I.V.E places us where they do, but here we are together. I know you never wanted to leave your family, but you aren't alone. Your aunt is here."

"Yeah and that's what concerns me."

"Why would your aunt concern you?"

Tessa hesitated, wondering if she could trust Arica, "One of the last conversations I had with my mother was about her sister. She confided in me that her sister was an Evo and that H.I.V.E took her away."

"Tessa that's absurd there aren't any Evos here in the H.I.V.E. Norine can't be an Evo. It must have been part of the dream."

"No. It was a real conversation because it was the same conversation as when I told her I was an Evo."

Arica rolled her eyes, "Tessa you are starting to scare me. You are certainly not an Evo. I've known you all my life, and I would know if you were an Evo."

Tessa concentrated on the now empty coffee cup just as she had the pen in her room. It began to quake on the table, and Arica pushed her chair back in surprise. Tessa held her outstretched palm toward the cup focusing harder pushing past the fog, and the mug levitated off the table. Arica stood up in fear and backed away from the table.

Tessa put the cup back down on the table, "Don't be frightened. You were frightened the first time you saw me use my powers in our real world as well, but this isn't the first time you've seen it."

"I don't understand. The H.I.V.E doesn't allow Evos here."

"I believe you, but here I am. So why? What do they want from me?"

Arica sat down still tense, "How can they take your memories? How can they take my memories?"

Good. Arica believed her, "I don't know, but the doctor is insistent that I take these pills." She took the pills from her pocket and handed them to Arica. "Is there any way you can find out what these are?"

"Yeah in the lab but I'll have to wait until I can get some private lab time."

"I think that would be best. It would be better for both of us if we kept this all between the two of us."

"But I want my memories back."

"And we will get them back, I promise. There is something big going on here, and I intend to find out what. Once we discover what it is the H.I.V.E is hiding here, we can stop them and then make our escape."

20

Both Tessa and Arica tried to continue about their days as though everything was fine. They pretended everything was fine and a sinister government organization wasn't working to alter their memories and use them in some nefarious purpose. Trying to act natural while believing everyone is conspiring against you isn't an easy task. At least Tessa could blame it on the fake amnesia diagnosis they had provided her. She had a reason to act awkward. She wondered what excuse Arica might be using.

Tessa spent the whole morning in her lab trying to pretend to focus on her work. What she was actually doing was watching every person in the lab like a hawk and analyzing their every action. Maybe someone would slip up, and she could figure this puzzle out. But everyone remained in character and nothing seemed out of the ordinary. Then again she wasn't sure what ordinary was here in the H.I.V.E. She was like a fish out of water and didn't care for that feeling at all. Tessa was always planning one step ahead of everyone. Here she felt like she was last in the race.

Tessa kept a pen and paper in her lab coat pocket, and occasionally she pulled it out to jot a few notes down. Most of them were scribbles and mental rants as she started to form her plan of attack. Her brain was filling up with conspiracy theories and extraction planning. She had to start putting some ideas on paper so she could make room up there for more thoughts. She had to plan out the details precisely since she was living in the lion's den. One false move could have deadly consequences not just for her but Arica as well. She was beginning to outline a plan and making a checklist of equipment she need to pull off the job.

When the lunchtime bell rang, Tessa couldn't wait to get to the cafeteria. She was eager to meet back up the Arica since their morning revelation. The two girls walked through the food line in silence as they collected their lunch, both terrified that someone would overhear them. They managed to find a table in a back corner which offered the most amount of privacy. Tessa smiled on the inside for a moment almost chuckling. Despite everything that had happened to them, it seemed like some things never change. In school, they had always sat at the back corner table, and here at the H.I.V.E, they were no different. The H.I.V.E might try to change their memories but who they were at their core could not be changed. They were always the outcasts. The outsiders.

Once they felt their conversation was secure, Tessa asked in a hushed voice, "What did you find out about the pills?"

"Nothing good. They're a neural inhibitor."

"What's that mean?"

"It means the pills dampen your neural activity. It's why your mind feels foggy, and you have problems accessing cognitive functions including your abilities."

"So don't take the pills. Got it."

"Won't they know if you don't take the pills?"

"Haven't taken them in the last twenty-four hours and no one seems to have noticed. I still feel foggy though."

"It might not just be the pills. They could be weakening you for some other type of cognitive manipulation. It's hard to say. It still doesn't explain why I don't have my memories and instead, I have these fake memories."

"We'll figure it out." Tessa dug in her pocket for the supply list and slid it across the table to Arica, "Speaking of figuring things out. I have a plan on getting the stuff they took from us, figuring out what exactly what they want with us, and getting the hell out of here. That's the list of supplies I need to make my plan work."

"Tessa some of this stuff is going to be hard to come by. A management tablet? How are you going to get that without anyone knowing?"

"I have an idea for that one, but let's save it for last."

For the next few weeks, Tessa and Arica went to work in the labs as usual. They were always waiting for that perfect opportunity to snatch up an item they needed from the list. They had to be cautious that no other lab techs witnessed a theft and there was no eye in the sky to catch it either. As it turned out, Tessa was pretty good at sleight of hand. Arica, on the other hand, required some practice, and at least Tessa could teach her.

Arica had always been a pure soul. She had a good-natured heart, and it was difficult for her to break character with her inherent nature. Tessa wished she didn't have to corrupt her innocence, but right now Arica was her only ally. They had both come to the conclusion that her aunt Norine couldn't be trusted. Both girls got an odd vibe from her when she visited. Norine always asked bizarre questions making them question her loyalties. Tessa just had to figure her loyalties lied with the woman Tessa caught her kissing in the hallway, who she later discovered was the Director of the H.I.V.E Science Division. Tessa thought a leader like that had to know something about why she was here and what she was working on with the Tesla coils. It was possible she was the one behind it all.

Tessa and Arica slowly whittled away at their list and squirreled their treasures away safely in Tessa's flat. She had discovered a loose ceiling tile where she could easily stash the items away from any prying eyes. She wasn't sure how secure her room was, and it was best to assume the worst and hope for the best.

The last item on the list was the management tablet and Tessa's whole plan revolved around that piece of the puzzle. It was a critical part of the plan. The tablet would grant her inside access to aspects of the H.I.V.E that could help her gain admittance to secure areas and information needed to discover H.I.V.E's motives. The basic plan was for Arica to distract Elissa the lab secretary long enough for Tessa to palm her tablet and clone it to a spare one from the lab storage closet.

The two girls began to execute their plan strolling into the lab office ready to strike up a conversation with Elissa. Arica started the conversation, but their target seemed preoccupied and disinterested. Arica was losing her attention too fast, and their window was closing. So Tessa took matters into her own hands. She focused, pushing through her mental haze and seized her power. It wasn't much, but it was enough for what she needed. She concentrated on a shelf which housed glass lab beakers filled with a variety of lab chemicals. More specifically she focused on the brackets which were holding up the rack.

Tessa managed to break the shelf brackets with her power causing the chemicals to tumble off the shelf and crash onto the floor. Not only was there now glass and chemicals everywhere in a sterile lab environment but Tessa had hit the jackpot. The mixture of the compounds spilled started to form a chemical gas cloud that sent the lab into a panic. Elissa ran from the desk and into the lab to assess the situation. Tessa seized the moment to slid her tablet off the counter and into her lab coat pocket. She nodded to Arica to keep watch while she slipped around the corner to the storage room.

There were no cameras from this vantage point. Most of the cameras were focused on laboratory entrances and inside the individual lab suites watching over research projects. There was supposed to be someone always manning the laboratory reception desk and monitor lab supplies in the closet. With a gloved hand, Tessa jiggled the door handle and found it to be locked which wasn't a surprise. She concentrated again and gave the handle a swift, forceful downward push, and she heard the lock break.

Tessa snatched up the first spare tablet she saw, firing it up. The seconds it took for the tablet to boot up and synchronize the cloning process seemed like hours as the alarm sounded in the lab. Tessa could begin to smell the chemical cloud from here. Her eyes began to water and her nostrils burned. She slowly started to cough as the chemicals tickled her lungs. She peeked around the corner to see Arica nob her head giving Tessa the signal that it was time to go. People were evacuating the lab, and it wouldn't be long before a hazmat team would arrive to clean up and re-sterilize the lab.

She wrapped up the cloning sequence and on her way toward Arica placed the original tablet back on Elissa's desk. Tessa glanced around to see if anyone had noticed. It looked like they were in the clear with the cloned management tablet tucked safely into the interior pocket of her lab coat. Now with all the materials collected Tessa could return to her flat to begin preparing a plan to figure out what was going on here and how to escape this nightmare.

The first thing Tessa needed to do was get her stuff back. She needed her goggles and the electronic device Finn had given her to contact him. She needed some help, and he was the only other person she trusted. Before she could do any of that she had to make sure her wireless connection to the tablet was encrypted and masked so that she could work incognito. She wanted to make sure the tablet operated in stealth mode, and if someone were to go sniffing around, they would have a hard time tracing the original signal. So she routed her access signal through thousands of other access points from other tablets or computer workstations within the H.I.V.E. It took some time to make sure she had the device configured correctly, but it was well worth the wait. It was useless to even to start their mission if they were destined to get caught within the first hours or days of beginning. Tessa didn't nearly have the same tech-savvy as Finn, but she knew enough to be dangerous.

Once the tablet connection was secure and untraceable to Tessa's standards, she began her research through the management files. First thing first, she had to access the camera network for several reasons. She wanted to study the movements of high ranking H.I.V.E personnel and directors. Her primary targets were the Science Division Director, Dr. Fang, her lab director, and her aunt, Norine. They were all hiding the truth from her, and she was hoping to at least discover some clues as to what and why. Tessa figured some movements in their daily routines might solve some pieces to the puzzle she was working on inside her head.

The second perk of having access to the camera network would be the ability to manipulate that network. If Tessa wanted to move around within the H.I.V.E undetected, the first checked box on to her to do list was to control the camera network. With the right connection, she could loop video and mask her covert movements from the eye in the sky.

Tessa spent the next few weeks meticulously watching and waiting while she formalized her plan of action. She had discovered that her aunt was in a romantic relationship with the Science Division Director. That confirmed Tessa's thoughts that her aunt was literally in bed with H.I.V.E and working against her. She also discovered the location of her missing belongings. The items listed in a confiscation manifest list within the management files, housed in a secure room on the upper management floor. All she needed was an access badge, and she had already collected all the tools she needed to make one.

As Tessa trolled through the H.I.V.E inner workings and computer files she came across a folder titled "Top Priority Projects." The title was enticing and could potentially answer questions about Tessa's project and why it would be important enough to construct such an elaborate ruse to ensure her cooperation. Inside the folder were several other folders with another folder labeled "Tesla Project." Within the file, Tessa found the details of her supposed H.I.V.E project. The most intriguing find was that no details were mentioned Tessa at all within the project's notes. That only confirmed in her mind that she had not been working in the H.I.V.E for months as everyone had claimed.

There was another file folder that caught her attention and piqued her curiosity it was titled "Project Genesis –Director Clearance." Tessa tried to access the file but received an automatic denial. The restricted data was encrypted, and it was far beyond Tessa's ability, but if she could get her stuff which contained a communication device to contact Finn he might be able to help her. There was a sinking feeling deep in her gut that this Project Genesis might be the motivation behind all of H.I.V.E's endeavors.

21

Tessa crept through the dimly lit hallways, as Arica sat in her room watching her progress on the tablet. They had successfully looped video of an empty hallway for anyone watching the eye in the sky camera feeds. But Arica could monitor the hall in real-time. She could look ahead and make sure Tessa didn't run into anyone on her journey to the confiscated item storage.

The containment storage was where the H.I.V.E collected the belongings of people assigned to the facility. Specific items were not allowed into the facility from the outside world. When assignees reported to the H.I.V.E; management reserved the right to confiscate items upon arrival. Arica had explained that process to her. For some reason, Arica remembered her arrival and the process of integrating into the H.I.V.E.

Tessa never received an assignment to the H.I.V.E in the first place, and her items stolen from her just like her memories. She refused to accept their deceit and wanted her stuff back. Tessa wanted more than anything to be free of this place, and she would make sure to secure her friend's freedom at the same time. She still had a curious itch wanting to know why the H.I.V.E would establish such an elaborate charade to keep her in the dark about the truth, including her Evo powers. Surely they knew about her powers; they at least knew that they needed to suppress them.

They needed something from her. She just had no idea what that something might be. If they needed her Evo powers, then why suppress them? Maybe they only needed her engineering skills. The bottom line was that two plus two did not equal four. Nothing was making any sense.

Tessa planned this recovery mission in the early hours of the morning so there would be fewer people moving throughout the H.I.V.E. This particular floor housed management offices, which at this hour were unoccupied. However, she could still run across custodial staff, although it was unlikely. Arica could be her eyes and give her a heads up if that might be a probable encounter.

Tessa reached the steel storage room door with the security card access lock. She pulled her fake security card badge out of her pocket. It wasn't just a card. It had wires running from the card's security chip to a handheld computer decrypter she had made from the supplies they had collected from the lab. The decrypter not only ran through an algorithm to open the door with the chip but it also scrambled the record of the door opening log. Tessa was careful to cover her tracks. She inserted the card and waited for the red light of the decrypter to turn green.

Tessa slowly turned the door handle and slipped into the room quietly closing the door behind her. The lights in the room automatically turned on, and Tessa could see the room. On the far side of the room, there was a vertical conveyor belt with shelved compartments attached to them. It looked like the conveyor belt ran deep down into the facility and upward as well. The compartments visible were the size of a large shoe box, ten wide and five deep and ran from wall to wall and floor to ceiling in the room.

To the left of the conveyors was a computer station built into the wall with another security card access port. She inserted the card and let the decrypter work its magic. Once she was in, she searched her name in the database and selected the compartment. The conveyer wined and started the move vertically on its track until it stopped and her assigned compartment was visible. She opened the container and removed the contents, checking to make sure everything was accounted for and stuffed it into her backpack once she was satisfied. Then she retrieved Arica and Sam's belongings and secured those away in her backpack as well.

Tessa retraced her steps and left the storage room taking her security card decrypter with her. She was cautious to move the conveyor back to its original position. She carefully traversed the same hallway path back to her room and reconvened with Arica. Both girls were elated at being reunited with their belonging from the outside world. A hint of sadness plagued Tessa in thinking about home. Back at home, her sister Evie was no longer alive. H.I.V.E murdered Evie, and Tessa would never forgive them for that transgression. Her hatred toward the H.I.V.E motivated her to discover the truth behind the curtain and expose and destroy them all. She would dismantle them from the inside out if she could manage.

Tessa rigged up her goggles to the tablet so she could use its comlink. She connected Finn's communication devise, and within a few seconds the tablet screen scrambled with fuzz and materialized into Finn's face. "Thank god you answered! I need your help."

"What? No Hi Finn, how ya been? Long time no see."

"Honestly I don't have time for pleasantries. I'm stuck in the H.I.V.E."

His expression turned from playful to serious in less than a second, "Hold on." His face disappeared, and the static fuzz returned.

Arica had to ask, "Did he just hang up on you?"

"No." Tessa paused, "I don't think so." She wasn't sure. Maybe he did. She could understand why an Evo would want to steer clear of H.I.V.E.

His face returned, "Okay, now we're good. You did a pretty thorough job masking your connection, but I went ahead and tweaked it just a tad to make doubly sure no one can listen in or locate the source."

"Thanks that's one of the big reasons I wanted your help, but I had to get my comms and your connector to establish contact."

"How are you at H.I.V.E?"

"They were home waiting for me as you said. They murdered my little sister Evie."

"I'm so sorry to hear that." He offered his condolences, and so did Arica. This moment was the first time she learned of Evie's death. The trauma was still so fresh in Tessa's mind, and she wasn't ready to talk about her loss. She hadn't had an opportunity to grieve. She was busy trying to get out of the H.I.V.E and figure out what was going on and why.

"They didn't do any of those things you hear stories about. I woke up in a hospital bed, and they tried to pretend that I had been working here for months. They made me believe that my old life and my Evo powers were some elaborate dream I invented while in a coma."

"You were in a coma?"

"Not really. Their story was that I electrocuted myself while working on a laboratory experiment."

"What did they say you were working on?"

"Tesla coils and Aether power."

"That's interesting. I wonder what they want with Aether power."

"Your guess is as good as mine. Whatever they're working on here its big, and get the feeling it can't be good if they're willing to go to such lengths to succeed. I'm not sure what their end game is here, but I'm hoping you can help me figure it out and then get us the hell out of here."

"Us?"

"Yeah, us. The H.I.V.E took my friends Arica and Sam too. You remember them from the rebel base?"

"Yeah, I remember them."

"I guess it was a way to make their lies seem more believable if there were people here that made me feel more comfortable."

"That makes sense."

"My mother's twin sister is here too. But she seems to be loyal to H.I.V.E. My Evo abilities are suppressed. They gave me a neural inhibitor drug, and I stopped taking it. I can reach a fraction of my power, but it's not full strength. I'm not sure what's blocking it."

"Well, we will need to get to the bottom of everything to figure this out."

"I ran across a computer folder about something called the Genesis Project. I feel like that might have something to do with what is going on here."

"Sure. Hold on and let me take a stroll through their network." His face disappeared in the fuzz again for nearly ten minutes and then returned. "Looks like if you want me to help you access those file, you'll have to at the Science Director's office computer."

"How hard is that going to be?"

"I reviewed the schematics, and it's not a walk in the park, but with me nothing is impossible."

"Alright, tell me what we need to do."

They talked for hours over the best plan to extract the information. There wasn't enough time to complete the entire mission plans in one night. Tessa would have to make it through another day before she had any final answers. At the very least that gave Finn more time in the network to troubleshoot the perfect plan.

Tessa and Arica floated through the day in an exhausted haze, but the promise of answers was worth losing a little sleep. Their quiet lunch was interrupted by her Aunt Norine who joined them. "Ladies, how are the projects going?"

Tessa nibbled on her food as she responded, "Still trying to get my bearings. Not sure what they want out of this research."

"A clean, viable source of energy."

"Right. But for what exactly. The Tesla coils produce energy enough to support the facility. It seems like it's not enough. They want more. What for?"

Arica wiggled in her seat. She wasn't expecting Tessa to interrogate her aunt. Norine answered but it was vague, "They want to make sure there is plenty of power to sustain the vitality efforts and re-establish a growing human population. Why so many questions Tessa? Are you still having problems with your memory?"

"You could call it that."

"I know it's frustrating but the doctors here are the best, and they believe that eventually, your memories will return. Until then follow their directions and keep to your work. Have the pills been helping?"

Why would she mention the pills? Did she know Tessa had stopped taking them? "They help."

"Good. Keep taking the meds, and maybe we can get you back to your old self." Norine finished her lunch and left the table.

Tessa and Arica gathered their food trays, and as they were walking through the cafeteria toward the garbage can, she felt an odd little tickle inside her mind. She couldn't quite describe it, but it felt strange like it shouldn't be there. She tried to pin it down and when she did an excruciating sharp pain radiated throughout her mind. Her tray crashed to the floor, and she grabbed her head in her hands in agony. Arica was trying to speak to her, but she couldn't focus on the sound of her voice. All she heard was every sound in the cafeteria amplified a hundred times. She could hear people chewing food, talking, even breathing all at once. She could barely see through blurring vision. The fluorescent lights seemed to burn her eyes as she struggled to regain control.

When the episode subsided, Tessa realized that everyone in the cafeteria was staring at her. Arica helped her pick up her tray, and they tried to leave the room in a hurry, but Tessa was stopped by a few orderlies requesting that she visit the doctor. She reluctantly followed them and walked past Norine standing in the exit doorway. They locked eyes as Tessa walked by and held that eye contact as Tessa looked back over her shoulder.

Tessa figured that Norine knew she wasn't taking the pills and reported her to medical personnel. How could she know? Tessa had been so careful in hiding her symptoms. And what was that mental pain? How did that happen? More importantly why and what. She wasn't sure what IT was. All she knew was that it hurt like hell. She wondered if there was technology here that could probe her mind. Could the H.I.V.E have planted a device inside her mind? Whatever it was it had to be responsible for her Evo power block or at the very least related.

In the med bay, the doctor gave her a full workup and had a laundry list of question about her memories. When the bloodwork came back, he confirmed that she wasn't taking the pills. "Why are you not taking the pills, Tessa?"

She had to think of a believable lie and fast, "They make me sick to my stomach."

"You have to take them if you want to get those memories back. Take them with a meal, and they won't hurt your stomach so much." Did he believe her or was he playing along? "If I can't trust you to take your meds, you'll have to stay here under observation."

"I'll try to do better." Tessa took the blue pill from his hand and put it in her mouth chasing it with a glass of water the orderly handed her. She did not want to end up in observation. That would delay her plans to get out of here for good.

Tessa left the med bay and headed back toward her lab. Along the way she found a single stall bathroom and proceeded to evacuate her stomach by shoving a finger down the back of her throat. It took her a few times, but she managed to get that nasty blue pill to come back up and more importantly out. She might need her Evo powers for their mission tonight. Not to mention the fact that Tessa refused to let these people control her.

When she returned to the lab, Norine was waiting for her. "Feeling better?"

"All patched up." Tessa shrugged it off. She had no desire to speak with her traitorous aunt. As far as Tessa was concerned, she was no different than her H.I.V.E enemies and deserved to be treated as one.

They worked in silence through the afternoon hours until it was time to call it quits. Norine invited her and Arica to dinner, but Tessa made up a story about a nasty headache and that she just wanted to have dinner in her room. Her aunt seemed disappointed but didn't press the issue. Tessa didn't want to spend any more time with her than she was required. She couldn't be trusted. Tessa was running out of time. They knew something was up with her, and it was only a matter of time before they figured out what she was plotting.

22

Arica jumped. Startled when Tessa charged into her room. "Is everything okay?"

"No, it is most definitely not okay. They really want to make sure I'm taking those pills. Is there any way for you to fool a blood test that I'm taking them?"

"Maybe. I'll work on it."

"Good, maybe that can buy us some time. When will Sam be back?"

She shrugged, "Couple days."

"When he gets here we need to bring him up to speed and make our move. We are running out of time."

Arica nodded her head in agreeance, and they started preparing for the evening's mission. Tessa ran through a review of all her tech components making sure everything would operate as intended. They patched in with Finn, and he started running them through the details. And he left out no details. He had spent the entire day combing through every inch of the H.I.V.E network, and at this time he knew their system better than they did.

Finn planned to guide Tessa through the mission over the commlink, and all she needed to do was follow his instructions. He walked her through retrofitting the security card encrypter so that he could tap into the tech. He could hard link into any of the security locks. There were fewer risks if Finn could access security, break the system, and cover their tracks.

They waiting again until the early hours of the morning before beginning. Arica remained behind as backup and Tessa started walking toward the elevators. She used the security card encryptor to access the management floor like last time, but there was another step. On the management floor, there was a special secure elevator designated only for directors.

She inserted the card, and the light turned green. A display screen to the right of the elevator requested a retinal scan. Finn accessed the security through the card encryptor and bypassed the retinal scan. The elevator door opened, and Tessa stepped inside. She was about to find out the answers to her questions. She was nervous and scared but also excited. Butterflies were swirling in her stomach, and her palms were sweating.

The door opened, and she stepped out into a hallway running to the left and right. Finn guided her through the corridors and past empty offices where H.I.V.E directors worked during the day. Now the rooms were dark and uninhabited. Finn's directions stopped in front of an office at the end of the hallway. There was a gold plaque on the wall the right of the door Director of Science, Dr. Marlize Sharron. With Finn's help, she unlocked the office door and inside was the secretary's office. Tessa needed the director's computer, so she passed the secretary's desk and proceeded to the door behind. Finn had to help her with this door too. One thing was clear. H.I.V.E took their director's security very seriously.

Tessa took a seat at the desk in the oversized leather chair and plugged Finn into a port on the central computer. She had to stand by while he hacked into the computer. It took longer than she expected and sitting in the dark room alone didn't help her anxiety. She browsed the room for intel on who this woman was. There weren't many photos at all, and most of the trinket in this room were trophies. She had awards in many fields, but most of her accolades seemed to be in genetics. More specifically Evo genetics.

On a wall was an old photo of a group of scientists holding similar awards. On closer examination, a plaque below the picture dictated a caption: Gruber Prize in Genetics, Yale University 2153 Dr. Jonathan Sharron; for an evolutionary advance in the human genetic code. One of the men in this photo must be a relative of the director. And judging by the caption they were at the forefront of the Evo creation.

Finn came over the comms, "Tessa I'm in, but you're not going to like what you find."

"I never thought I would."

The transparent holographic computer screen projected above the desk and Tessa started inspecting the contents of the Project Genesis file. Finn started to copy the drive so that if they need access to the information again later, they would have what they needed. Tessa found a list of names in the folder and she open a couple.

They were all Evos. There were photos, bios, listing power, genetic code, and video including footage of their capture and in some cases torture. The most haunting information she found in the files were cell numbers and videos of violent experimentation. She found documents evidencing that the testing was to develop and weaponize Evo powers.

She didn't have time to sift through them all, but she stopped when she found her name. In her file, she saw footage of her capture and sadly Evie's death. It was hard for her to watch and tears rolled down her face as she relived that moment. But at least now she knew that moment was real. They couldn't take that from her.

Tessa was not assigned a cell, but they marked her as a high priority asset. She drilled down through her file to discover that they believed her psionic power was the key to getting the Aether experiment to work. They thought that her deep connection with energy would allow her to make a breakthrough in the technology. There were details of her integration into the H.I.V.E. She received drugs to inhibit her from reaching her full power. They only wanted her to access a portion of her ability. Just enough to complete the Tesla project. She was too dangerous to be allowed to access all her power.

She found detailed memos from the director to Dr. Fang in the Tesla lab. Dr. Fang was to ensure that her lab would play along with the amnesia ruse so that Tessa could work on the projects. There was memo after memo with directives on interacting with her. The whole H.I.V.E knew who she was and was expected to continue the amnesia dialogue.

She confirmed her aunt's involvement. Norine was assigned as Tessa's liaison. She was assigned to monitor and report on all of her activities and ensure that she worked on the Tesla project. Later in the memos, Arica and Sam were brought in to make the whole lie more believable. The manipulation of her friends was H.I.V.E's desperate attempt to make her feel more comfortable while working for them.

Now she wanted to know why the Tesla project was so important. The specs of the project were to provide a sustainable power source. As she read through the specifics, she could hardly believe them. They needed the power to fuel a gigantic space vessel. Not a space vessel, an ark. But the H.I.V.E wasn't planning on taking two of every kind off the planet. They intended only to save humans. They would leave Evos along with the plants and animals of Earth to perish. Not only that but they weren't even planning to save all humans or even an ample cross-section of the population. They were only taking the elite with them.

They were using the labor of other humans to build this machine so that the high ranking H.I.V.E management could escape Earth. They planned to traverse space until they found an inhabitable planet to colonize or one that they could terraform. There were details of other science projects on terraforming and other pertinent subjects. All those scientists developing that technology would be left behind.

Tessa located the engineering schematics for the ark and at the top of the page written "Project Genesis, a new beginning on a new world." There were several versions of engineering specs and some amendments were recent and notated encountered problems with the project. That meant this wasn't just an idea. They were building it. How far were they in the process? And where were they building it? It would be far too big of a project to keep it confidential here. There had to be an alternate location.

It only took a few minutes of flipping through folders before she found her answer. There was a secret level here in the H.I.V.E base that only certain high ranking officials were privy. The director's elevator shaft was the only access point. There was a subway tunnel with a tram that traversed underground from Cheyanne Mountain to the Denver airport. There underneath the airport, they were building their ark.

Finn finished his copy of all the files and Tessa headed back to her room. She was nearly in a daze from the information overload. These people could not be allowed to continue this work. They were vile human beings, and they should not be the ones to survive. They should not represent this planet. Tessa knew that this project had to be stopped no matter the cost.

She no longer wanted freedom only for herself and her friends. She had no choice but to free the captive and tortured Evos. No one should be left to suffer for this cause. Right now she was the only one with the knowledge to stop this atrocity. She had to save everyone who lived on this Earth.

Made in the USA
Columbia, SC
26 September 2021